City Swimmers
& Other Stories

Steve Clark

BLACK NOTE
PRESS

MADRID 2024 NEW YORK

Copyright © 2024 by Black Note Press

All rights reserved.

No part of this book may be reproduced in any form or by any electronic or mechanical means, including information storage and retrieval systems, without written permission from the publisher, except in the case of brief quotations embodied in critical articles and reviews. Please send requests to Black Note Press, 50 Montrose Road, Yonkers, NY 10710.

ISBN (e-book): 979-8-9904167-0-3
ISBN (paperback): 979-8-9904167-1-0
ISBN (hardcover): 979-8-9904167-2-7

Cover Design by www.onegraphica.com

for Yulia
Sasha & Oliver

Contents

For the Love of Wasabi Peas   1

City Swimmers   13

A Small Yellow Space   25

The Revenge Fund   33

Pizza Thanksgiving   47

His Day at the Beach   55

Strange Beds, Strange Houses   69

A Last Stroll through Her Favorite City   83

Aren't You Glad I Called?   95

The Reunion   109

For the Love of Wasabi Peas

She stepped through the revolving door, took a left into the bar, walked to the round glass table in the corner and sat next to him. He looked, as they used to say in places like this, *smart*—when your clothes were right, together. He did that semi-stand as she sat, still, even after thirty years of friendship or whatever you call the existing force between two people who've been married and divorced twice to each other, and then married again. It seemed, now, their third conjugal *hoorah* was coming to an end.

It was unclear whether either of them cared. Besides an unfathomable knot of—what was it? (emotion, attraction, taste?)—they didn't know why they were together, except for a locking sense of humor, a degree of love (whatever that was) and a *blood-wise knowing* that they were somehow meant to be. Also a look they found of themselves in the other's eyes, from time to time.

A martini appeared on a tray, which was something for 3 p.m. on a Tuesday. He nodded it over to her and signaled for another.

No matter how popular the place was, how many friends lived in the neighborhood (though they didn't), you still didn't run into anyone on a Tuesday early afternoon; so it was unusual that fifteen minutes later, a man came up, one of those clubby types, who speaks loudly, never has an uncombed hair unless he's dissolving in a steam room (his wisps springing like stringy eels), stopped at their table. She was a quarter through the martini. They were arguing about something.

"Hey, buddy. Don't want to interrupt, just saying a quick hello." The man's hand opened over the table like a bar of soap. Always such manicured hands, these gents, fresh and dainty like rolls of mulberry silk. Before he shook, he knew it'd be cool and firm, accompanied by very direct eye contact that'd been stamped into his irises by god knows how many generations of grandmothers who smelled like salty rocks.

"Ah, there he is," he said, because he knew him well but didn't have time to do the half-stand. They must've had dozens of friends in common; they'd drunk together hundreds of times, been to the same parties as children; but he, even with all that, wasn't confident enough to say his name. The wrong one—after what? 35 years of acquaintanceship—would've been more than a slap.

She hadn't stopped talking because she was wrapping up her argument, teetering toward a point. "And I do know about boats—"

"You know my wife," he interrupted. "She knows everything. Even the things she doesn't know." He lifted the glass to her. "In fact, the things she doesn't know, she knows them more."

The guest paused, then nodded to her. "Of course." The man wasn't sure what to make of them. Were they drunk? (The answer? He, almost).

He stood there and grinned, waiting for a cordiality so he could politely leave. He did not receive this.

"I know my husband's an ass. Virginia. Nice to meet you."

They had met maybe forty times.

His smile tightened.

"Likewise."

They'd been arguing about a moment over the past weekend, their last fight. He'd been idling the dinghy toward a rocky island in Maine, and she was telling him where to drop the anchor. But the lock on the outboard was broken so he couldn't lift it; he had to stay deeper. She'd said, "It's sandy over there, go that way." And he'd said, "It's too shallow, please jump off and I'll back it off." The current was pushing them toward the shore, causing him to reverse from time to time as she stood on the little bow, talking to him. "Please just get off," he said. "I'll anchor back a few feet." He didn't want to ding the propeller.

"Why not there? You always brush me off."

"My god, just please. You don't know what you're talking about."

It was true, she had never driven a boat; she certainly didn't know the draft of this particular boat (or what a draft was); and as she kept arguing, the chances of damaging the propeller were increasing. But she kept talking, "I'm saying over there is better. It's sandy."

"It's too shallow. Please, let me deal with it."

She had finally jumped onto the beach; and with the hood of her yellow slicker flapping in the wind, she turned, red-faced, yelled at him for never listening, for belittling her, for waving her away (as he always did!), and stormed down the beach to sit as far away as possible. All the yelling got swept up in the wind, so he could only gauge the anger by her expressions, which (in the last six minutes) had gone from placid, pleasant even, to that of a little, steaming bull. *There goes the afternoon,* he thought. *Another Saturday.*

Why had they married three times? Twice—okay, one makes mistakes. But to walk down the aisle with the same person a third time is inconsiderate. Well, *walk down the aisle* is misrepresentative. They did the third mainly by paperwork, and then sent out a card to fifty friends that said: *We screwed up. Cocktails for our third pitch. Highballs and Home Runs.* They signed it *Mr and Mrs* with the date and address. The party had been fun; the past two years less, but not entirely shit.

The problem with going back with an ex is you realize your mistake faster each time. The little things that bothered you don't go away. The foibles, the habits. They just bother you more and faster. This is compounded by your awareness of the stupidity you've displayed in believing that love can change love. The first marriage had been seven years, the second four, and they were just coming up on two with all the familiar dread. Late autumn made it worse. Everything was dying beautifully. Acid notes in the pre-winter air. Like dread. Like death. *A deathy anxiety*, he'd called it.

That's probably why they met here; if they were going to end it, it might as well be a soothing place, one that contained not only their plush memories but those of thousands of strangers, perhaps hundreds of thousands. They coated the place with a pallor of forgetfulness. Like morphine but legal. And more decorative. Same bartenders, drinks. Surely, that must count for something. Also, they were too old to nuzzle up to friends for consolation; and anyway, a drink was better than a pal asking if you were okay, which to be clear, they both were.

His eyes followed the man as he walked back to the bar, slapped what appeared to be a junior colleague (birthday? promotion?) on the back a little too hard and reached for what looked like the last watery sip of a scotch.

"That was pretty," he said.

She sipped her martini and her eyes gathered to a green point.

"Do you think you ever loved me?"

"I do love you," he answered. "Even though we're hell together."

"I'm not talking about *that* love. The love of *we've known each other forever, I don't want you to get hit by a truck*. Not that familiar love blah—"

"I get it," he said.

But she didn't stop.

" . . . *We're family, I don't like you but I have* to—" He raised two fingers to a passing waiter. She didn't notice as she inhaled, "Not the love that's just shared time." She suddenly realized her purse (did they still call them *purses*? Maybe it was just a bag) was unbuckled. She buckled it and looked at him.

"I married you three times," he said.

"Oh c'mon, that doesn't mean anything."

"I'll tell the priest."

"Fuck the priest," she said sharply.

They were silent for a moment.

"I just want you to tell me the truth."

"The truth? My god, what d'you want me to say?" His tone became dreary; he was worried it sounded too dreary. "It's not that complicated. We fell in love. I asked you to marry me. We married. That's it. We did it a bunch of times."

"That's not it. That's just the point. Everyone thinks that's *it* but that is exactly *not* it. Just because people do it doesn't mean that is the thing; the thing is what makes them do it."

"Aristotle would disagree."

"Are you kidding? Aristotle?" She was suddenly about to cry. "Fuck you." She stood up. He stood up with her and took her hand, which she yanked away, but he again reached for it more tenderly. She let it sit. At that moment, he didn't know if he was trying to calm her or prevent a scene. It was probably 50-50. He said, "I'm sorry." She was angrily fiddling with her scarf, a brocaded expensive-looking thing. He said, "Okay, let's talk." He sat. He was wondering if she'd sit too. 50-50. Reluctantly, she did, but not before saying, "You're a real shit."

The waiter took the glassy triangles, now empty, placed down two more. The slender ice chips floating like paradise. He drank the first sip, still able to lift the full glass to his lips without spilling a drop. Not drunk at all.

Might've been the third martini or the possibility of looming rupture (breaking up!) that made him feel the world was filling again. He felt he was about to fall—no, jump!—off a cliff into a new adventure, and he wanted to, but didn't; and not knowing whether he'd actually leap filled him with a removed glee, which, neither pleasant nor unpleasant, was at least a change. It made him feel *casi vivo,* as they say in Spanish. She, on the other hand, felt they were about to stumble off that same cliff, but she was pissed at the cliff for being a cliff, and him, for being the callous jerk who invented this cliff. It was annoying, tiring. She thought, *I've fallen off three fucking times. Is there at least something I can learn?* She thought, *Maybe yes, maybe no* as she stared at him.

"I'm just trying to have a regular conversation; I'm not trying to fight." She said this as she thought, *Who is he? I know him exactly as well as that stranger over there or that other one in the stupid hat.*

"I don't want to fight either." He had to bring it all down; if it was going to end, it had to end down there, the lower registers.

They both leaned back at the same time. The synchronicity of movement was unintentionally (and for him, unwelcomingly) funny. It wasn't the right time for the confluence of laughter. As they stared at each other, well-knocked stakes in the dirt, they were both aware of the laughable futility of being here yet again, stubborn, middle-aged idiots. An involuntary smile, like a help line, curled from her lips, but she pulled it back before he could take it. Not because she knew he wouldn't (he most likely wouldn't) but because she had other things on her mind.

Things that, to her, were, at this moment, more important than relationships. This relationship. Who cared anymore about that? Strident, nebulous forces were driving her. She needed to figure something out, even though it might be intolerable. Like picking the lock of the diary of someone you know never loved you as much as that other one *(the one!),* the one who left them. And you gave yourself so fully. They were your *the one.* The urge to pick the scab, knowing you'll scar. You can't not pick it, it's screaming at you. *Do it.* She had this running through her, like bad water, and needed him to filter. He was clear-eyed, more simple, an American purification system. No toleration for dirt. For *not knowing. We can know it all in time,* etc, etc. He would sop up all that crappy blood, the doubt, the dumbness of it all; and the truth, or contradictory gold, would pour forth. Back to her. From his eyes, his mouth. She would know something. She would learn.

"Do you want something to eat?" he said.

"No."

She lightly pinched the skin below her Adam's apple and steered the bit of flesh down a curved mountain road. He'd noticed this nervous habit (was it nerves?) with others and told himself he'd study it when he got home. (He never did.) Abruptly, as if reading his thoughts, she folded her hands in her lap, wiggled in her seat and became very tall while shaking her head.

"We all want this thing which is a lie, but it's why we do everything we do. Isn't that just—" she shuddered. He had never seen her shudder. "Just . . . incomparably sad."

"What thing?"

"My god why are you so thick!"

She flung her knuckles at him and pulled the air back at her chest frantically. "This, you idiot. This."

She stopped and stared at him. He didn't move, then started out slowly. "*This* is not everything. Sometimes *this* . . ."

"God, I know that. I'm not talking about us. Don't worry. That's done. I'm talking about what it means."

Done. He rotated the word in his mind, trying to feel how he felt.

"Why does it have to mean anything?" he said.

"Because it does. It does. Everything everyone is doing all the time—working, studying, fucking, joking, breathing, shitting, dieting—we are all doing because we want this thing—"

"What goddamn thing?"

He felt he had to raise his voice to calm her. She said nothing; he looked at her. Involuntarily a line of Shakespeare went through his mind: *My mistress' eyes are nothing like the sun.* Maybe because hers now glowed like burnt-out suns, beautiful chunks of black coal. His expression became serious.

"Why do you think loving someone is a lie? It's not a lie."

She listened to that.

"The urge to love isn't a lie," she said. "The rest is."

"It's not . . . It's not." He didn't know why he'd repeated himself.

In the next minute, it became certain to both of them. The conversation was over; it was all over.

He looked at the ceiling, then clambering for a latch, he rested his palms flat on the table. "Listen to me," he waited for her to look at him but she didn't, so he went on. "If you believe that, then you have to reach as deep down into yourself as possible and lie your face off, telling yourself it isn't." She kept looking down. "Otherwise you have nothing," he said.

She raised her chin.

"At least it's a true nothing."

"A true nothing is still nothing."

The waiter had approached the table, was asking if they wanted anything else. She looked down.

She doesn't remember getting up or looking at him as she left. Only walking out, stepping into the revolving door, and pushing until she was encased by the curved glass. She stopped before she was outside. The silence of the rotunda around her for longer than just a moment. Neither inside nor outside. Neither here nor there. As if in a snowy poem. The street milky, a few shuffles away. Behind her, the round small tables, and who could count how many days? How many days. She placed both hands on the brass push-bar and leaned forward, but the door didn't move. When she turned, in his own pie-slice of the door, he was there. Only the wing of glass between them. Still smart, together, a blue scarf wrapped below that familiar face. It was the game children play when they hold the door so you're stuck. It had once given her claustrophobia, but now it just was. A sad playfulness danced in his eyes. She wasn't sure what he saw in hers. Expressions don't matter all that much. He lifted a finger to his ear, and she leaned forward. Someone had started to play the piano inside. It wasn't their song or anything like that, or even one they knew, just a line of falling notes, that caught each other, and then carelessly wandered off. Apart, together, together, apart, together apart. Maybe the song was someone else's. A request.

Over her shoulder, a black sedan pulled up. Most likely, someone coming in for a drink, dinner. It seemed, in their life anyway, a black sedan was always pulling up. As she looked at him, she realized she'd asked the wrong question. *Did you ever love me?* That wasn't right, it wasn't even close. He watched her intently (she seemed she might say something). He felt what had moved in his eyes roll into hers, and maybe that was enough. It was enough. When you fall in love, no matter how old you become, how many years pass, a part of you remains that age for each other forever, no matter what. She had wanted to ask, *Do you remember that bar on Canal Street, the one with the four-leaf clover in the window?*

CITY SWIMMERS

1.

This is a story about a run.

He runs. Pages fall behind him with the changing leaves. Mental scribble. Knots in the plot come loose. He's trying to figure out the story.

Clara on the 6 train, picking at a mosquito bite on her left wrist. She pulls into Astor Place but decides to stay on a couple more stops.

The sweat has just broken through the center of his black T-shirt, where the triangle of his ribs meet. *The xiphoid process,* he thinks, and wonders again why names often have little to do with what they name. Below a hammer-shaped cloud, he runs farther down the West Side Highway until he's at the tip. He turns north, the buildings stacked, adamant spires. Back to his story.

Where is Clara going? Who is she? She's a woman who doesn't believe in god, but prays.

The sun has been up for two hours. He picks up the pace. Sasha will still be asleep when he gets home; the croissants will be warm.

Disheveled, with his straw bowl cut, Sasha walks into the kitchen rubbing his eyes, the hunger bell in his stomach. He is six, bleary, serious.
"Papa, what's that?"
He knows the answer. Every Friday. The white paper bag next to a vase of old sunflowers on the kitchen table.
"I have no idea."
"Papa, seriously."
Sasha crinkles the bag open. "Did you get it?" He looks up and his mouth widens with his eyes before he dives in, saying, "Almond."
He digs under the puffy regulars until he finds the squeezy one, observes the sugary, paper-thin nuts as if jewels plucked from a Harry Potter bog, walks to the kitchen island, pulls his favorite blue plate from the drawer, comes back, sits and stares at the beauty in his hand. It's as big as his face.

"Papa, are ghosts real?" He's half-through the croissant; the grip of his hunger has loosened into curiosity.
"I don't think so."
"Then why are they all over the place on TV?"
"Probably cause they're scary."
"If a ghost came up to me, I'd cut his head off."
"All right."
He's rotating the pastry in both hands, looking for the next mouthful.
"The ghost wouldn't mind, because it's already dead."

"You have a point."

"Papa?" He picks off an almond that displeases him. It has joined three others on the blue plate.

"When we die, do we become ghosts?"

"I don't think so."

He licks some powdered sugar off his top lip.

"Georgie says we go to heaven. That god lets us in. And we live in the clouds."

"She does, huh?"

"Especially kids. If kids die, since they're kids, they go straight up." Sasha puts the croissant down and looks at his father. Nikolai has been watching him eat, the meticulous, almost surgical attention.

"Is that what happens?" Sasha asks.

"What? Heaven?"

"Yes?"

"I don't know."

Sasha speaks as he chews. "You *should* know, you're older than Georgie. She's only 13."

He waits a moment and swallows.

Nikolai isn't sure if you'd call his look *eager*. "No one knows, Sash. Lots of people will tell you they do, but they don't." Nikolai looks into the greens of his eyes. Hard to count how many greens. He smiles what he hopes is a reassuring smile and that Sasha believes it, and says, "Anyway, not knowing makes it more exciting."

Sasha holds this thought, then tosses it. "No. Georgie's right. Because they're kids. They go straight to heaven."

Nikolai nods and shrugs. "Some people think that."

"Because it's true," Sasha says.

Nikolai leans over, pinches the little knob of fat between his eyes, where Nikolai's mother used to kiss him.

Sasha squirms. "Stop!"

"Go brush your teeth."

"Wait, what about the other one? The regular one."

"Okay, but sneakers on in ten minutes."

Sasha digs back into the bag.

"Thanks, Pops."

"Make your bed."

Nikolai walks to the bathroom, back to the story.

Clara has left. So fast, after so many years. But why? They have children, a boy and girl. Twins, almost ten. It's not that he'd cheated on her, though he had five years ago; and not that she'd cheated on him, though she had three years ago . . . Ugh, no, that was all drab, why was he always writing about break ups? No, Clara was on the train because she wanted to explore a part of New York she'd never been, although she'd lived her whole life there. Scratch the kids, scratch husband. Clara was older. Seventy-five. Never married. Not a cheater. Not an artist, not a writer, not a reader of books. He'd used too many of those types. Who was she? Why did she want to suddenly explore the New York she'd always lived in?

Nikolai wraps up his two-minute shower, dresses and finds Sasha by the front door finishing the knot on his right sneaker. He learned the bunny ears a week ago.

"Beat ya," says Nikolai, disturbing Sasha's knot.

"No, you didn't," Sasha says without looking up. "You're wearing slippers."

"I certainly am."

"Slippers aren't shoes."

"Slippers *are* shoes. The best shoes. I'm wearing them."

"You are not!" Sasha shrieks.

Nikolai opens the door, and they walk down the hall.

Clara walks down the hall.

Moments ago, she'd gotten off on Canal. Walked down Baxter past Pell Street. Sat in a playground. Only a few kids.

Wednesday, 8:15 a.m. Then stepped into a few tourist shops. Listened to the language she couldn't understand. The man behind the counter had a fixed look of survival, like any shop owner who depends on a worthless product. She'd walked into a six-story building with large panes of dirty glass, past an unattended desk, and followed two Chinese girls into the elevator. She'd gotten off on the fifth floor after them and now she walks down the hall.

Clara walks down the hall.

At the end, there's a bright, rectangular light, the uneven striking of piano notes. Some smiley faces on the door and a sign in English and Chinese that says WALTER'S MUSIC CLASS. Some paper cut-outs of piano keyboards, musical notations, violins and drums. The two Chinese girls walk in, say hello and sit outside one of the booths with the foggy glass. Clara greets the vibrant lady at the desk and asks about violin lessons for her granddaughter. She wants to give them as a gift. How old is she? Has she played before? What days would work? Once, twice a week? After they've exchanged the information, Clara says she'll email her, but instead of leaving, sits on one of the fold-out chairs. The lady at the desk smiles and drowns *back into her computer, scheduling. There must be a drum lesson on the other side of the glass because Clara can hear muffled thuds. She closes her eyes. Just for a moment, she says to herself.*

Sasha and Nikolai don't take the subway. Unlike most New Yorkers, and Nikolai is a born New Yorker, he doesn't like the subway. Its hot airy convenience. The yellow, aquarium light. Suffocation. Cabs are worse. The suspension so low, more rake than transport. Then the myriad car services, where the drivers, with their friendly smiles, would drive you into the East River if their GPS told them to. No, they walk. It's forty-five minutes, much of which Sasha spends on Nikolai's shoulders pointing out boats below the Brooklyn Bridge. *Look! A tug like the story. Is that a freighter? How many Pete the Cats do you think are crossing the Atlantic today? Cargo ship.*

At the apex of the bridge, Nikolai puts Sasha down. He feels a drop of sweat glide down his sternum. It's pleasant, the weight of parenthood. He gives Sasha a quick kiss at the classroom door. Sasha heads to his cubby to hang his backpack.

On the way back, Nikolai walks over the Manhattan Bridge to vary, complete the loop, strides down the concrete onto Canal Street. Only now he realizes he has walked for over an hour in slippers.

He notices he's in the same neighborhood where he left Clara. Where she is in the story. Their neighborhood. She's dozing in the music school only a few blocks south, the lady behind the desk watching her. He will not go see her. Not today. He turns north. He needs to get home. He walks faster under the scribble of the yellow awnings. He's anxious to get back to his desk and put Clara onto paper. He has held her for so long. Her thoughts. They need to be hammered onto the page or they'll blow away, and she'll never have existed.

Never have existed. It was like that. If you don't write it down, it's like they never were here. Never were real. But she did exist. She was real. Her brown eyes, her lemon wrist. It'll be three years in December. Sasha barely asks for her anymore.

2.

This is a story about a lake.

The lake, with its toothpasty smudges of early light, is cold but not unswimmable. She clasps her hands in front of her, presses up on her tiptoes twice, raises her arms into a skinny triangle and dives off the dock. She swims toward the center of the lake. She had swum the 200-yard freestyle at the University of Michigan, just missed the Olympics by a swim cap. She jets out at full speed, sleek, perfect, a half-submerged submarine. Sasha watches cross-legged from the dock. He's wearing his helicopter pajamas, and trimming his stuffed cat's toes with scissors from a Swiss Army knife. The sun hasn't yet broken through the magenta clouds.

She's far away now. But every minute or so, she stops and looks back. Sasha can swim, but you never know. She's almost two years in, still learning. She hopes the baby's sleeping. He's a good sleeper, so is Nikolai. She can get away with this morning perk. Nikolai likes waking up with the baby on weekends.

She swims through the blurry reflections of the houses on the other side of the lake. At a second-story window, she turns and starts back. She doesn't like getting too close to the other bank. It's shallow, foot-slimy. On the way back, she's faster, stronger; her muscles recall the shape of their capacity, her college days. Last night, when they were eating pizza on the picnic bench, Sasha had said, *May you pass me the water?* (He was always saying *may* instead of *would*.) And when she'd poured him a glass, he'd said, *Thanks, Mama*, and drank. Sasha hadn't noticed the slip, but she and Nikolai had. Or had he meant to call her *mama?* She and Nikolai shared a look, and her chest had pulled at her throat.

Her body's almost back after three months. Her stomach muscles reuniting with their counterparts at her center. She loved being pregnant; besides a little fatigue, she was built for it. No morning sickness. And notwithstanding the burning euphoric 30 minutes of pushing-pain, the ring of fire, she wanted more. She wanted to be a mother spaceship, dropping baby souls all over her garden. Her breasts were full for the first time. When they'd made love two nights ago, at the height, her nipples shot out milk. They both laughed. A translucent spurt had hit Nikolai's shoulder; and she, laughing but also embarrassed, had wiped it off. He'd caught her hand and said, "I want to taste it," and put her finger to his mouth. "Just like I thought," he laughed.

They had lain there quietly with the baby in the crib and the boy asleep in the other room. The autumn stars bright and cold outside the wood-paneled glass.

"Let's have another," she'd said to the window.

"Whoa there, hotdog."

"I want to be pregnant all the time until we're done."
"You want an army of swimmers."
"Not an army."
He kissed the side of her forehead. They had slept eight hours.

She hoists herself onto the dock; Sasha has her towel ready.
"Why thank you, sir."
"You're welcome."
She hops on one foot, tilting her head, then the other, a habit from her swim days, then picks up Sasha, though its getting harder, presses him against her, kisses the corner of his eye. "Do I feel cold?"
He smiles and shakes his head. "I'm not a baby." He worries he's hurt her feelings, which he has but only for a moment.
When she sets him down, he says, "Thank you." And then staring at his feet, "I'm going to be seven and a half in two weeks."
"I know, I'm sorry. Sometimes I forget you're such a big boy."
"You can kiss Pete."
Sasha pushes his stuffed cat up to her mouth.
She kisses Pete where she kissed Sasha. "Guess what I'm making today?"
"I think I know," Sasha says.
When she only raises her eyebrows, he says, "Say it. Say it!"

Nikolai sits at the table. His thin hair stands up as it always does, the wispy strands in a state of permanent static electricity. Usually, a baseball or cowboy or ski hat would be on to avoid the comb, but now his coif is in full Jack Nicholson mode as he looks down at the baby pressed to his chest, whose deep blinking eyes take them all in. When she gets closer, the baby whimpers, raises his pudgy hands. She can't help but pick him up. A sound from the infant as she kisses his stomach. Sasha goes to the cupboard, takes out four dishes. He sets them on the table. His father grabs his wrist, pulls him close, "I got you." He pokes his rib, squeezes the tight skin. Sasha can't help but smile before he breaks away, back to setting the table. "Where are the juice glasses?" he asks.

Once the table is set, Sasha sits on the counter, watching her make the French toast. The smell has started, and he nods briefly at her from time to time as she flips one piece then another, yellow to brown. The pan fits three at a time, and he already has his eye on the largest piece.

* * *

There's an unusual amount of early snow that winter, but the temperature can't hold it. A series of mornings where the sky is dark, shifting chunks of granite. It's on one of these mornings, another Saturday, while they eat pancakes, that they tell him. She's pregnant again. Nikolai does the talking as she tennis-balls her eyes between them. Sasha manages to smile because he knows, even at this age, that's what's expected, but he can tell by his father's changing look, and hers too, especially hers, that whatever's happening on his face is not giving them joy. They watch him. He looks down, he's only halfway through the first pancake, and takes another bite, but it's alien, funny. He feels tears, but doesn't want to ruin what they clearly think should be a happy moment. He doesn't want to cry; he's seven and a half now and then some. He's saved from this small humiliation because the baby knocks over a glass of orange juice. Nikolai lifts him from the high chair and pulls him to his chest. When he turns back, Sasha's gone, out the kitchen door. They watch him run across the lawn from the window. He reaches the end of the dock, stops, slightly out of breath, and jumps. It's January lake water, but he swims a few strokes, then doggy paddles back without getting his hair that wet. When he pulls himself up on the dock, she's sprinting, holding a towel. His father trails behind holding the baby. He can see their terror-stricken faces. She's about to cry, if not already. She almost tackles him with the towel, swooping him into her arms. She's strong and rubs him all over as she holds him close. Her breath smells like maple syrup. A few seconds later, Nikolai arrives; he stops, watches them. She finishes with the towel and holds his shoulders.

The sun has broken through, laying a sharp, gold vein over the lake. They are silent for just enough time. When she wraps the towel tighter around him, Sasha steps forward and hugs her. He knows she needs him to do this. Not for too long, though. He lets go, grips the towel, closes it over his chest. The baby squirms in their father's arms, and Sasha starts to walk back to the house. The sturdy line of his back, the straw, damp hair. They follow, forming a triangle. Nikolai at the back right, the one connected to all the points.

As they walk over the snowy patches of grass, Nikolai isn't thinking of the baby in his arms, or the one in her stomach, or Sasha. One day, when it's too late, Nikolai will think of all this, but now it's her. At some point, he will have to meet her. He knows what the story is about; he's not someone who doesn't know what the story is about. Sasha will be old enough then. Sasha will say things. When will it happen? When will they meet? The notes, the yellow walls, the music class, Clara asleep in the chair.

A Small Yellow Space

"Why can't I?" said Maude.
"You just can't. One thousand percent No."
"I don't see why. I really don't."
"First of all, it's beneath you; second of all, I just don't see how I can look at you the same if you do. And that'd be a shame; I like looking at you."
He did, especially now. She was sitting at the kitchen table, early, prismatic light coming in from the garden window in their Lower East Side apartment. It was his favorite time of day, and it was late August, which made it better, with the birds (their song heavier now) and exhaust of trucks, both heading somewhere important, even though it was Sunday.
"But I really really want to."
"Nope. Nuh-uh. No way."
She had one hand scrunched against her cheek while staring down at a large glossy book. You could just see her eyes under her black bob, shiny as a Cadillac, his favorite mole where her philtrum and lip met. She was wearing a sleeveless V-neck, and something about the shape of the shoulder, the round brownness of it, made him want to take her back to bed.

A SMALL YELLOW SPACE

"I'm doing it," she said.

"For the love of god, No!"

She slapped the book shut, which now you could see was a cookbook, walked by him and started digging in the freezer.

"Maude," he said her name, which he never did, since they had a million nicknames for each other, but he did it for emphasis. "Maude, no one puts plums on a pizza." She had pulled out the frozen dough and was unwrapping it on the counter. "No one in the history of human existence, not even bored emperors' wives or Louis the XVI or Marie F"ing Antoinette ever even considered putting plums on a pizza."

"Oh, it's happening, baby."

She grabbed the glazed bowl (their five-year-old had insisted on the bright, almost radioactively bright, orange color before painting it at the kid pottery place). It was filled with plums, and she placed it in front of her, possibly for effect.

"This is a sad, sad day," he said.

"Go wake up Leon. He's going to love this."

* * *

When he comes out of his shower, sure enough, Leon's sitting at the counter next to his mother, slicing the pitted plums with a mandoline. He doesn't get a chance to speak before Leon says, "Papa, we're not letting the plums go bad, you might as well help."

"It's not a rocket ship."

"Get the prosciutto out of the fridge," Maude tells him, then to Leon, "When did your father become such a crank?" Leon smiles, the dimples are nuts.

"Fine. Fine. Fine."

He has the package of meat in his hand when the landline rings. He looks at Maude but she only stops momentarily, stares straight ahead, then returns to carefully placing the sliced plums on the mozzarella.

"Want me to answer?" he says after the third ring.

She nods, still at work.

He steps into the little office, stares at the old phone stuck to the wall like an ivory mouse with a curly tail, picks it up, sits at his desk. "Yes, I'll accept," then after some crackling. "Hi, Malachi."

"Maude? Maude?"

Malachi's voice is an agitated wound or a knife but comes through the receiver small, comical, though he's anything but. He imagines Malachi as a tiny man talking into a large cup.

"Put her on, Billy. Just two minutes."

Billy exhales. "She doesn't want to talk you."

"I know, but just two damn minutes."

A moment of silence.

"She's busy."

"Doing what? I mean, doing fucking what?"

"I'm going to hang up."

"Why'd you pick up in the first place? Why didn't you let the phone ring through like a decent person?"

Billy chuckles. "Malachi, we all know I'm not a decent person."

"You're a real prick."

"Ah, the pleasantries, we're in the middle of some important stuff here. What is it?"

"Why bother asking?"
"I'm not asking for me."
"She can't ask herself?"
"Ok, hanging up real soon."
"Get Maude."
"Bye bye."
"Wait." Billy feels Malachi unleash a silent groan. He imagines Malachi's soap-opera chin and wavy, all-over-the-place hair. It was a damn good-looking family, you had to give them that.
"Promise you'll give her the message?"
"Why do you think I picked up? There are other things I could be doing on Sunday morning." As he says it, he realizes there's nothing else other than watching the culinary catastrophe in the kitchen. "Come on, spit it out, man. Don't have all day."
"You can formally apologize to her for me. I formally say I'm sorry. Tell her that."
"Fine."
"You didn't ask for what?"
"Call me a genius, but I imagine it's for blowing off your mother's funeral, leaving her to do all the talking and handling, and besides that—"
"Hold on there, Genius. I'm NOT apologizing for that."
Billy stares at the phone. You couldn't tell if he was bored or interested.
"No, no, no, no," Malachi groans. "Not for that. That was necessary. I'm proud of that."
Billy shifts in his chair. "Of not going to your mother's funeral?"

"Yes, I am. I'm not a goddamn phony."

"All right, buddy. You been reading *Catcher in the Rye* again? You're what—38 years old? Get a fucking grip. I don't care how you felt about your mother, you show up. Even if she'd sent you to Auschwitz, you show up for your mother's funeral. And even if you hated her that much, you don't let your little sister handle all the mess. You BE a man, and handle it." Billy's surprised at how worked up he's getting. He probably shouldn't be saying all this, considering, but he can't help it. He finishes with, "Jesus Christ, you're like a moral infant. Wah, wah, wah."

Billy's heart's beating pretty fast when he stops, and surprisingly there's silence on the line, but then he's more surprised when he hears sniffling.

"Are you crying?" But the sniffle gets louder, and he realizes Malachi's giggling.

"You're fucking laughing."

"First off, I never read Catcher in the Fucking Rye, alright Hemingway? Secondly, you're wrong. If you didn't love and actually hated someone, even if they are your mother, you don't show up like Saint Gabriel at their funeral pretending death absolves. I want to go and listen to everybody tell me what a wonderful woman the old bag was and then hear about how god is wrapping her up in his gooey arms? Give me a break. And anyway, none of this is the point—"

"Love if you got to it then, don't have all day to chit chat."

"Okay, then let me get a word in, hot shot." Malachi pauses to see if he will. He continues, " What I want to apologize for is . . . Do you remember the old FAO Schwartz?"

"For the love of god."

"Do you?"

"Yes, the one on Fifth in the 50s."

"Exactamundo. Well, we were there one day buying a toy for my ex's kid. She was turning four, and I wanted to get her something she'd like. You can imagine I'm not exactly the type who'd know what a four-year-old girl would like for her birthday, so I asked Maude to come along, which she did, and we picked out this cute doll in a flannel shirt or something. We were in a hurry because I'd left it to the last minute, and the birthday was at some Serendipity-like place on the Upper West Side. I was making Maude come because the girl loved her, even though she barely met her, so even though Maude was supposed to go meet friends for brunch, I convinced her. Anyway, I started to get really impatient because she was slow, was wearing these sort of low boots with heels. I kept making her walk faster, telling her we'd be late and that we couldn't be. She kept saying, *Why don't we take a cab?* and I told her it was just across the park, and of course a little uptown, that it'd be faster if we'd just walk, which she did, and faster too. Anyway, it was about a 22-minute walk because we did it speedy, and the kid loved that Maude was there. We even made it on time. But after the kid blew out the candles, I found Maude in a corner with her boots off, rubbing these big blisters. I guess she wasn't wearing socks, and she didn't tell me. She wasn't mad, but why didn't she mention the socks? I mean, who wears boots without socks? But tell her I wanted to apologize for that; I should've sprung for a taxi."

The line was silent. Two men pretty much the same age, phones pressed to their ears.

"That's what you want to apologize for?"

"Yes, that's what I want to formally apologize for. Formally."

"Okay, I'll tell her. Bye, Malachi."

After he hangs up, Billy sits in his chair a moment. When he steps into the kitchen, the pie's in the oven, Leon's playing with magnet tiles, building some kind of airport, and Maude is looking out the window. He walks over and puts a hand on her shoulder. She asks the question though she knows the answer.

"What'd he say?"

"Same as last time."

THE REVENGE FUND

It's the loudness that makes her shift back and forth in her high tops, not the humiliation. This is what she tells herself. The smash of the night crowd, their sharp, tipsy voices—that's the issue. She'd act the same if this wasn't happening. They are on the other side, her three friends. Their pretty faces, pretty heels. They wave their hands around him; they entreat, palms out and apart, as if reaching for a baby, while they snap their glossed lips. They emit energy, distaste, anger. He doesn't budge. They'd be taller than him without the heels, but still look like they belong at the same feast. They, at least now, seem less with her, more with him, this button of power, though their demeanor and words project the opposite, that they are on her side. He's beautiful in his way, a turkey vulture in a gray suit and black V-neck. You could bounce a quarter off him. That he is not young, that he's most likely her age, makes it worse. It's not frivolity that excludes her, that keeps her on this side of the velvet rope, this smiling noose; it's been thought out. He looks over their bobbing heads, scans the nightly glob vying to get in. Her friends cajole, plead, but they are only motes of dust for him, angry motes certainly, almost beautiful; but have no effect. He looks like he's about to smile.

They usually went to a bar where they could talk, but one of them wanted to dance (fucking Celia with her pointy tits); and suddenly they were all on the way. Usually, she would've gone home (she hated clubs, the volume obliterating her strongest assets: voice, intellect, humor.) But he was coming, and he knew she knew he was coming. It was mild enough when they'd met through Camilla, one of the select on the other side. A work friend of hers. They'd run into each other on Prince and Spring, had all gone for a drink. He was just out of her reach, but smart enough to notice and give her time. Shy and alluring behind his tortoise-shell prescriptions, there was that glint. Of course he'd take an interest. She was the smart one, the funny one, the driven, the one who'd succeed. Who knew about books, film, philosophy. The other girls too, yes, they were smart, independent, modern women, but when push came to shove, could rely on other natural gifts. Camilla had kidded her after he picked up the tab, how long they'd talked, rendering her, more or less, invisible.

When he shows up, she still has not crossed the rope. She watches him notice the girls over there hoping to pull a golden string. Trying to part the stanchions for her. She knows he knows what's happened. He frequents these places enough to understand but not to affect. He smiles as if he doesn't know what's happening. The kindness of that. The kindly shape of his eyes. He says, "Hello," and she's recharged momentarily. This is all of no consequence, in the larger scheme (she knows this), though against her will, her cheeks and chest burn. Having him see her like this. "Hello."

The man in the gray suit breaks away from her attacking gaggle, her pretty champions, unclasps the rope, and a group of five or six, a shiny cluster, pulsates by her . . . Hair, teeth, victory. As the pulchritude struts in, two dudes fist-bump him. His colleague, the other man working, a sleek Jamaican, whose job also is to unclasp, gestures back at the girls, the consort of anger simmering by the entrance, says, "What's up?" The buzzard doesn't think she can hear him, says out the side of his mouth, "Face Control." He's referring to her. It's her face that's being controlled. Being excluded, shut out. The colleague looks at her. Does she detect sympathy? A crack in the hard stance, this Saint Peter of the night? Perhaps for a second, but then he's searching the crowd. Back to work. The vulture walks over to her friends; and she's sure he's telling them they can go inside or leave. Though she heard the two words, *Face Control*, she's quite sure he hasn't. She hopes. She looks up, looking for escape in his attentive eyes. He takes a breath, and she knows he's going to say, *Let's go somewhere else*, but that'd be admitting what has happened has happened, and she can't. She quickly raises her cell like a badge, and points to it, loudly shows her friends, *I have to go*, but they come toward her, struggling against another flashy influx. She calls out, "I really have to go!" They're coming to leave with her, but she'll not have it. She says something fast to him, hopes he'll let this moment die quick. *I have to be up so early*. Something like this, she says, and apologizes, as she darts thankfully into a cab whose door has just vomited forth another burst of party people.

In the cab she feels relief. Relief the knife was not twisted by his disguised pity. She shakes it off, but tries not to feel rage toward this other man, the commander of the rope. She knows it's not him specifically; it's business. She does not add to the business model, does not contribute; in the loudness, where all is surface, she somehow costs them; and he is there, the buzzard, the whole festive machinery, is there, to make money. Who should she rage against? Soldiers don't kill the men who make war, only other soldiers. Pawns eat pawns. How she would like at this moment to kill him. To watch him die. *Face Control.* She knows this feeling is temporary. Tomorrow, she'll feel better. What will they have done? Hopefully they stayed. They did. She gets texts over the next couple hours. *This place sucks,* one of them writes. Where was she? Where did she go? They wanted to meet up. Later, it's Celia mostly texting telling her they all went home early. She knows it's true, though early for them is still two hours after her self-imposed curfew. They stayed, danced and drank. Who did he dance with? He doesn't write her. She doesn't expect him to. He doesn't even have her number.

Uncharacteristically, she turns on the TV. It's 2:30 a.m. She needs to be stupid, become numb. Is there not beauty and peace in stupidity? Relief from herself, that voice bullying her. The rejection in her cousin's eyes when they played behind the sofa. *I don't want to kiss you, you're ugly. So are you*, she'd said, and run to her mother's lap. *Am I ugly? No, my love, you are beautiful, and what's better you are kind. I don't want to be kind!* How the table around the cooling pasta in Spring Lake, New Jersey erupted in laughter. Those awful, grown-up faces. *I don't want to be kind. Hahaha. How few are pretty,* she thinks, *and how little it matters, but it does, even now that it matters less, it still does.* She stops on a channel in the high 100s. Something appeals to her about the mice in the cage, the guy in the lab coat. His groomed avalanche of saltpeter hair. It's all clinical, almost sinister. He's talking and she's not listening, but slowly, the whiteness of his coat, his measured tone draw her in. What she comes to understand is that he's been giving mice shocks, small electrical charges. Uncomfortable but not dangerous. He's discovered the mice have two reactions. Some receiving the shock just take it, they don't react. Others respond violently, attacking the electric wand or the other mice. What the scientist discovers is that those who don't react suffer disorders. They become listless, depressed even, don't eat. They lose the will to live. Those who lash out, thrive. She watches till the end, turns off the light and eventually finds sleep.

The next week an event happens that's as likely as lightning striking a tin can off her head, except even that would be more likely than what happens on a Thursday at 6:15 p.m., when she receives a phone call from someone whose name she doesn't catch. As it's so absurd, I will try to put it here as plainly as possible. Her father, who's been long gone due to an unwillingness to have a camera explore his insides, or any yearly check ups for that matter, due to a stubborn, irrational fear of modern medicine and doctors, had a first cousin (she was previously unaware of) who had no children but had become immensely wealthy due to a lucky marriage and maybe even luckier divorce. When I say *wealthy*, I don't mean duplex on Park Avenue, and never work again, but rather, *What building shall I donate to ease the suffering of mankind?* It's so shocking, she feels the urge to vomit; in ninety seconds she has become just shy of the Forbes 400 list. She feels heat in her feet, in her chest, as she makes the appointment to sign the paperwork in a lawyer's office overlooking Rockefeller Center. The deference this stranger on the phone, presumably a man high on the legal totem, is showing her is something she's not used to, but will come to, if not expect, find normal over the next years. She's suddenly *Mrs* not *Miss*. When she hangs up, she doesn't call anyone. She needs to let this settle. She needs to recalculate what this means for the next 45 or so years of her existence.

* * *

The stylish turkey buzzard, the doorman, has a name, a full name, though most know him by the one word. The door guys, they all go by one: *Flash, Jimbo, Tycoon, Rocky*. At night over the ropes, the eager crowd launches these monikers like flares (are they made up?), hoping to be rescued from the sea of aspirants. To be let in. Into the comfortable rapture, the social knife-play of flirtation, of conquest. His real name is long, benign. This was supposed to be a temporary gig, but the money was good, a percentage of the door, plus the perks: a degree of name recognition among the "it" people, the posh and celebrated. Invites to parties, etc. People were nice to him, at least the welcome residents of this nocturnal world who meant dollars, either by spending or drawing them in. Of course, there were the others, the ones who didn't belong and wanted to, who might, when they were drunk at least, prefer he was dead, insult him. One or two had spat at him. "Do you know who I am? Do you know WHO THE FUCK I AM? I'm calling [insert club owner's name]." Though they often didn't know the name of the real owner, but cited friends of friends. Of people inside. "Is so and so here? How about . . . blah blah?" It was all tiring, and now he didn't drink or party, so it was just work. The sensual perks? He had slept around enough not to care about that anymore. It had actually become a romantic minus. Finding someone who wanted to be with a guy who worked every weekend until 4:30 a.m. wasn't easy. Forty-two. Yesterday he'd Googled artists who were discovered after 42. Not many. So far on his resume? Classes at the New York Academy of Art. His work had hung in two student shows. But that was when he was thirty. After work, he forced himself awake by 12:30 p.m. Coffee and then "the studio," which was just the southern brick wall of his Chinatown loft. Dirty but enough space. These "mornings" were his favorite time of day. He didn't look at his phone until 3 p.m. (this was *his* time), then he might step out for lunch, meet a friend. On the two nights he didn't work—a date on one, his work the other.

A techy, twenty-something promoter had done his website in exchange for hooking him up with work at the club. So his work was up there, out there, wherever *there* was, which was most likely nowhere. There was little traffic. Big art collectors, gallerists, curators, came into the club; and sometimes, if it came up, casually he'd show his work to them on his phone. Nothing more than "Cool" and a pat on the shoulder. Fuckers. He imagined how stupid they'd feel when he had his retrospective at MOMA. They'd flock. The art world—most of it was just warm white wine, bad canapés and shite. His work had gone from figurative to abstract; and now he'd hammered LED lights with dimmers into the backs of his canvasses so he could control the shadows behind his non-geometric shapes. At night he'd walk his abstract hall of paint, eerily lit, like what he hoped was a modern Caravaggio. Every day, he swung from thinking himself a genius to a hack. He had sold two paintings, one to his sister, whose husband in Maryland (a lawyer) could afford the 5,000 dollars, and another at a discount, 2,500, to a dentist in Schenectady, New York. He was a friend of his uncle's. He had driven up to hang the painting in that sad waiting room with the old copies of *Time,* the smell of fluoride and bacterial plastic. He thought how lucky this dentist would be when he made it. This waiting room would be a destination, a New York point of interest. That money meant little to him; he pulled that in a week, tax-free easily. But that someone had wanted to buy it meant something. Sure, he was a friend of his uncle, but no one had made him buy it. Somebody paid for his art. And if someone did, maybe many would.

It was a few months later that our friend received a call too. A less stunning call than the other, certainly, but maybe more welcome. A director from one of the top five galleries, not the start-ups, the east village or Bushwick ones, but one of those blue chips with galleries all over the world. The ones where those who make it end up. She told him that she'd randomly come across his work online. She'd been researching him. Her team had too. Would he like to have a coffee? He looked her up after he hung up. There she was, a director, at the parties, with the big shots. When he meets her, she's thinner than her photos, somehow a little smaller, but elegant. Jeans, stylish mocassins, cashmere sweater. Understated, expensive watch. What were they called? Patek Philippe or Philippe Patek? He could never remember. A throaty English (is it English or just an "Art"?) accent. Back at his apartment, his studio, she looks at the work, observes, says little. After they sit, and he serves herbal tea in a mug, she looks at him, says he's Donald Judd with a painterly touch. He's combining light and paint in a way that hasn't been done before. Almost braiding them together, strands of different mediums, which are stronger entwined. Why hasn't he shown? He shrugs; he's been concentrating on work, not marketing. She points to one. It's called *Race Car*, and reminiscent of such (though still abstract). What one might think are the wheels are not attached. They emit light. She says, "Don't sell this one. I want it." He will hold it for her. They speak over the next three weeks, have coffee again twice. She's busy, but makes time. She's interested in him, the gallery is. He luxuriates in her intelligence, her knowledge of art, ancient and new. It's as if he's floating in a pool of cashmere and old books. He comes to her office above the gallery, meets two of her assistants. They have seen his work. They are fans too.

She convinces him to quit the door, dedicate himself fully. An artist needs to be one hundred percent. It's about character, dedication. *The world awards you publicly for what you do privately,* she quotes someone famous. He's inspired. This is what he's been waiting for. This professional nudge. He quits. He's dedicated, produces. She has not mentioned the show yet; but after three months, she tells him they are giving him one in the spring. It's fast, maybe too soon, but someone has dropped out; only 14 weeks to prepare, to select, to make it perfect. Because he's unknown, it must be perfect. She thinks he can do it. He says nothing as she casually runs through the guest list. There will be a dinner the night before for 200 people. He can invite 20, the rest of the spots are spoken for. Over the next months, she works with him closely, why this one is stronger than that one. She suggests a few smaller works too. *They are easier to sell. Most buyers are sheep, if the right person buys, they all buy.* Two weeks before the show, she assures him it will sell out before the opening. The press: *Artnet, Modern Painters, Purple,* they're all lined up. It will be cool, fun too. Not entirely stuffy. He's become a different person, who he truly is. It has paid off. He tells himself, *My work has led me into life.*

The day of the dinner, he wakes up early. He jogs along the Hudson. He's been eating healthy; he's strong, lean. When he looks in the mirror, he could be ten years younger. Last night he was in the space, making the last microscopic adjustments with her, two assistants and the hangers. *Let's not clutter the entrance. These two should be closer than the rest. Two inches to the left, a half inch back to the right.* They have chosen eight large pieces (eight feet by ten feet) and three smaller ones (four by four.) When he sees them all on the wall, and she leaves for a quick meeting, and the others are turned away, he sits on the floor and chokes up; he puts his head between his legs and hums to himself, his eyes closed tight.

"We're done," she says at midnight. He should rest until tomorrow. He also shouldn't come too early, he should create anticipation, let everyone wait for him. Not much, a little. The invitation says drinks 6 p.m., dinner 8 p.m. He should arrive at 6:40. Just shy of obnoxious. No one arrives on time anyway. He goes over the guest list in his mind, his list of 20, which was difficult because his mother and father wanted to bring all their friends from the neighborhood. He said that everyone else could come the next day but the dinner was different. It was business. He thinks of each of them, how they must think of him now. His father, who loved but didn't believe in him, all those conversations about law school: *something to rely on if it doesn't work out.* His sister has driven up from Maryland with her husband, and their two young boys. His grandmother and grandfather will make it though they are in their mid-80s. Their first big night out in ten years, since their 50th. He has hired a van for the family so they can all arrive together. Pool their excitement. What would they talk about on the way? He hasn't invited his art teacher from the Academy to the dinner, but they hadn't kept in close touch; nor the dentist in Schenectady, but they had RSVP'd yes to the opening the next day. That was fine.

After his jog, he meditates, tries to nap. What can he do till 6:40? He paces. He decides to watch a movie. *Basquiat.* He watches with tears in his eyes. At 4 p.m., he tries to nap again but just lies in bed staring at the ceiling. At 6:15, he gets up, showers and walks out.

He takes a cab, doesn't want to sweat, gets out around the corner. He wants to prepare by walking the block and a half. It's cool, March air; he's not going to sweat. He thinks of all the new faces that will look at his new face. Who he's become. Those legends. He's researched many of them, will drop comments here and there about acquisitions, artists they both like. He doesn't have to be nervous. She's sold most of the show. They like him already, and he hasn't met them. She has said he'll be pleasantly surprised with who's bought. She'll tell him tonight after the dinner. It's better if he's aloof, not concerned with sales tonight. He shouldn't smile too much. He thinks of how he'll talk about the art. *I'm interested in the interplay between mediums, light and prima material. It's a reflection of how I believe we are ... we are made of the gross stuff of our bones, blood, etc., but also a kind of spiritual spark, or at least that's what I want us to be, so that's what I create* (No, he stops himself, I should say, *that's what* I attempt *to create*) *with my art.* He feels good, he's ready. When he turns the corner, he catches his grandfather's profile as he walks in. The last of his family . . . Their van idles in front. Perfect timing. He will say hello to his family first; they are, after all, what's most important. He increases his pace. When he walks in, they are all there. His family. Fifteen of them. Also the five friends he's permitted himself, including an ex who broke up with him (long story, but this would impress the shit out of her). They all have a funny look as if they've entered the wrong space. His sister is typing into her phone, presumably to him. When they look up and see him, they smile. "There you are!" But he doesn't hear them.

Except for them, the room is empty. The works are gone and the lights have been ripped from the ceiling; they are in a construction site, not a gallery. Two bulbs hang from their fixtures, buzzing. The light is very white. In the center of the space, a fold-up table with an open bag of Doritos and a warm Tab. Nothing else. It had looked glorious and lit and freshly painted yesterday, just last night. His heart screams around in his chest before he dials her number. All eyes on him. What's going on? Her cell is disconnected. Between shaking his head at family members, he digs up the gallery's number, dials the hardline. Someone picks up, he asks for her. He's in the corner now, sweating, talking and talking, until they finally put him through. When she answers, the voice is different, higher, less of an accent. She doesn't know who he is. She thinks she's talking to a lunatic. She *is* talking to a lunatic. She hangs up. He looks at his phone as if it has dropped from an alien galaxy. He walks around touching the walls as his family stares. They don't understand, no one does. He tells them about her, but they are confused, not sure what's happening. (When he arrives home later, his works will be stacked against his southern wall, wrapped just like when they were delivered.)

No one would have noticed her. Why would they? A girl in high tops peering in. She wasn't in the doorway more than five seconds. Ten at most. It was all she had to see.

As she walked down Crosby Street, which was strangely quiet at this exact moment, one of those rare pockets of silence in a never-silent city, she thought, *Wouldn't it be nice if they'd kept the sodium lights? Why did everything have to change? It would've kept downtown more romantic like Paris or Lisbon.*

Pizza Thanksgiving

"I don't see why you have to be such pain in the ass—"
"Nice word choice."
"You know what I mean," she laughed. "And it doesn't hurt, everybody does it."
He started to raise a finger. "I don't like anything—"
"You got that right," she cut him off.
"—that goes up—oh c'mon, I'm not having this conversation!"
"After a certain age, you have to. Okay, Marvin. Seriously. The appointment is made."
They were sitting on a bench eating waterdogs with everything on them, light on the sauerkraut, watching Lila and Thomas skate below in Rockefeller Center. The rink had been open a week. It was the day before Thanksgiving.
"I'm not going. You made the appointment, you go."
"You're going. Even if I have to come and hold your hand."
"You're not coming."
"Of course I am. Someone has to pick you up."
"Why?"
"Them's the rules, son. You need to man up."

"*Picking up* is not the same as *going*."

She didn't answer; she correctly didn't think it was a question.

"You can pick me up," he sighed. "But you're not going to wait there while they do god-knows-what to me."

"God knows what!" She threw her hands to her cheek in a mock Munch scream. "You're such a New Yorker."

"Why do you always say that? I don't even know what that means."

"You don't know how to shuck corn."

He took a deep, deep sigh. "One night, that was one night. I'm not from Nebraska, okay?"

"Just saying."

"And P.S., if I wanted to, I could learn in about four seconds."

"If we paid some shrink about fifty bucks, we could get to the bottom of this; I'm sure these two issues are related."

He looked at her.

"The two are not related."

Lila and Thomas were holding hands and skating around the tiny rink dodging a swarm of out-of-control six-year-olds.

"So what'd Francine say?" Marvin asked.

"I don't know."

"How can you not know? We need a head count. If they come, we need another turkey. There's like eight of them."

"I'll call her when we get home."

"Screw that, I'm asking Lila."

"Marvin, don't upset her."

"I'm not going to upset her; her family's ruining our Thanksgiving. What's Francine waiting for, the last glacier to leak?"

"Has something to do with the father, I bet."

"Ah, god."

"Yeah, I know."

She smiled broadly. "Look, look." Thomas was holding Lila's hands as she skated backwards. They looked like an Ivory Soap commercial. She watched them do a lap; he kinda did.

"How old is Lila? Is she a year younger or older than Thomas?"

"Older," Marvin said, picking at a hangnail.

"But they're in the same class, right?"

"Yeah."

"I wish I had known you when you were in college."

"Wasn't much to know."

"Bull. You had all the girls running after you."

He put his arm around her.

"That's a crock." He took a bite of his hot dog. "I was running after them, still am."

She elbowed him in the ribs. "You're keeping that appointment; you're starting to make dad jokes."

The smallest smile crossed his lips. "Dad jokes."

"You are." She put her head on his shoulder. "You're a good father," she said, and he knew she was thinking about it.

He squeezed her shoulder. They were silent a moment, and he didn't know if it was better to say something or not. He never knew if people wanted to be soothed but reminded of bad things or if they wanted you to ignore the thing altogether like Robert Frost. It was better to soothe, he thought. "It's going to happen," he said softly.

"Yeah, well, the chances are . . ."

"It'll work this time," he said.

She wiped the corner of her mouth with her napkin, nestled deeper into his shoulder. A wind knocked some leaves around their feet.

"Do you think they do it in our bed when we're away?"

"Ava."

He could feel her chuckling into his shoulder.

"They definitely fuck in our bed."

"Yeah, well, if they do, I'm not crazy about knowing about it."

"Where did you lose your virginity?"

"Nope."

"Where?"

"If I answer, you're not allowed to say, 'You see.'"

"Where?"

"Mother's bed."

Now the laugh came from her stomach, was almost evil, delighted.

"Why? Did she have to help you?"

"Okay, that's the line. You just crossed it, lady."

She suddenly lifted her head. Thomas was storming towards them, a skate in each hand, his cheeks bright as tomatoes, tears about to burst from his eyes.

"What's going on?" she said.

A small gust parted his blond curls from his forehead; he gave the impression of a golden retriever, its nose out a car window, but not his eyes, which had aged fifty years.

"Let's go," he said.
"What about—" Ava looked around.
But Thomas was already walking toward Fifth.
They saw her on the far side of the rink. Her profile. The buttony nose and wallops of caramel hair, but something too stiff at the edge of her mouth. She had her skates slung over her right shoulder, was headed toward Sixth Avenue. They were in her peripheral vision; Lila was aware of them, she had to be, but didn't look over, even to wave goodbye or anything. She just kept looking straight ahead, still managing to almost bump into a lady stuffing a magazine into her bag.
When they got to Fifth, Thomas was sitting in a yellow cab, the door open. They said nothing on the ride home. Thomas was the first out of the cab on 61st and Lex, keys in hand.

Hours later, when Marvin came down, Ava was drinking a glass of red wine reading a recipe about sausage and herb stuffing on her phone. He sat next to her and took a slug of her wine. He spread himself all over the couch; she had to hip check his knee to keep some room for herself.
"Give a woman some space."
"I don't believe in space for you," he said.
"All right, Romeo. What happened up there?"
He took another hit of the wine and handed the glass back to her.
"Well, Thomas and I got to the bottom of the old male/female dynamic. I think we figured it out. All future generations can thank us for the milk that shall not be spilt, the fights that shall not be fought, and all love that shall be made." He crossed

his ankles on the coffee table. "In fact, I think Thomas and I will run for the Oval. Those other jokers wouldn't stand a chance."

"Please don't run for president," Ava sighed and leaned back, rotating the wine in her glass, staring at it.

"So he's in the woodchipper, huh?"

"Big time."

"I wish I was young again," she said. "So much fun."

"A real ball," he said, taking her glass and having another sip. "I don't think I ever cried over a girl when I was 19, poor guy."

"Get your feet off, Julia." It was true; his feet were resting on Julia Child's ample bosom. He lifted them and placed them on a glamorous photo book of swimming pools.

Ava leaned back into the pillows, her arms at her sides. She bit her lip and cocked her head. "The strangest thing happened to me last night at that Terminate the Turkey Party Lizzy took me to."

He looked at her, "Yeah?"

"I had had a few wine spritzers and a couple tequila shots but not that many, and suddenly, I was on a stoop kissing a guy whose name is apparently Sal." She crunched her eyebrows. "I don't think I would've remembered but Lizzy just reminded me. She called when you were upstairs. Do you think someone slipped me a mickey?"

He tilted his head, looked at her. "You kissed a guy named Sal? Last night?"

"Yes, apparently he's some college student who plays hockey for Dartmouth and was following me around all evening. He must've pounced when I was headed home."

He studied her and squinted. "You're aware that you're married to me, right?"

"Oh yes, very."

"Well, that's nice."

"What's nice, dear?"

"It's nice that you're aware of that."

She looked up at the ceiling philosophically. "What a weird thing to do."

"I'll say. How long were you kissing this gorgeous athlete?"

"Long enough, I guess. It's amazing that it would've totally slipped my mind if Lizzy didn't call just now and say, 'Hey, do you remember kissing that jock on the stoop last night?' I don't think someone slipped me anything; I felt totally fine this morning."

She looked at him for the first time. Not much had changed in his expression. "Are you pissed?" He was looking at that hangnail from before. "How do you feel about all this?" she asked.

"About you kissing Sal?"

She nodded.

"The truth?"

"If it's pleasant."

"I feel like going to Mariella's for a slice."

"Mariella's, huh?"

"The pizza place doesn't go around making doctors' appointments for me."

He gave her a wry look. She bumped his legs off the swimming pools.

"A hockey player from Dartmouth? You could be his moth—"

He caught himself, but that made it worse; it flopped, unsaid, in the air like a sloppy, fat fish.

They were silent a moment.

She laughed.

"Could I?"

After a while, she sighed, "I hope Thomas is okay."

"Me too," he said.

His Day at the Beach

His cell rang. Of course, it was her.

She didn't wait for him to say anything. As soon as she heard a molecule of breath, she said, "Walker? Walker, are you there?"

"Where would I be? This contraption's like a—"

"Shut up, Walker."

"Shut up? You know I hate that—"

"Shut up, shut up, shut up, shut up, won't you just shut up!"

Walker took a breath.

"Mighty had his first panic attack; he's really scared."

Yes, Walker's son was called Mighty, and he was still angry about it. Only someone named Marika would name their son Mighty.

"What happened?"

"We were at The Natural Store, he was eating his lunch and—"

The Natural Store, thought Walker, and said, "What was he eating?"

"What? That's not important."

"It is to me. What was it?"

"A sandwich. What does it matter? And he started really—"

"What kind of sandwich?"

She was fuming and got silent. Was probably practicing some ancient breathing technique she'd learned in a wellness class. It was effective though. He got quiet too.

"I don't know why I'm even calling you."

"Okay, okay, go ahead."

She started off again, measured.

"He started to shake and looked as if the earth was crumbling. I asked him what was wrong. He said, 'I'm having a heart attack.' Can you believe it, Walker? A heart attack? He's eleven! I hugged him; his heart was beating like a race car. Minty was freaked out too. Poor Minty! He ran around and hugged his brother, wouldn't let go. It was terrible, so terrible."

Yes, the six-year-old, the little artiste, was named Minty. He had nothing to say on this matter.

"We took him home and got in bed. I had him take some deep breaths with me. Will you talk to him?"

"Of course."

"I'll get him."

"Hold on a sec. What kind of sandwich was it?"

"What does it matter? Jesus Christ!"

"It matters to me. This is a delicate conversation and I'd like to have all the facts."

She thought for a moment, took another ancient breath.

"It was a number 3, multi-grain, Brussels sprouts, tofu and provolone."

"Tofu?"

"I don't think this has anything to do—"

"If you fed me tofu, I'd curl up with my mommy too, and she's dead! But if she were alive, and my mother was a tofu-feeding..." He went on for a good ten seconds until he realized he was talking to nobody. He dialed her back.

"Are you finished?"

"Put him on."

The phone went quiet. Walker sat up in bed, then he sat farther up and crossed his legs Indian style.

"Hey, Dad."

The voice was small, smaller than he remembered.

"Mighty. How are you, Boy? What's happening over there in patchouli land?"

"I'm good." Mighty burst into tears. "What's wrong with me, Dad? You think I'm dying?"

"Oh no, Son. No, no, no. You just had a visit from the ugly dog, that's all. There's nothing to worry about."

"Really?" he muffled through tears.

"He used to visit me all the time. Scared the crap out of me, thought I was going to die every ten minutes, but now look at me, I'm still here and full of vinegar. No one's taking me out, especially some chirping Chihuahua."

The boy grunted a little laugh. "Chihuahua?"

"Yes, that little fucker's not going to scare us." Then immediately, "Don't tell your mother I used that word."

The kid now really chuckled. "I won't, Dad."

"Good, good."

"I was really scared, Pop. I thought I was going to die; I couldn't breathe. I thought I was having a heart attack." Mighty seemed about to cry again.

"The good news is you're too young to have a heart attack. You just have to remember it's not dangerous; nothing bad's going to happen, it's just scary as hell. I know it."

"Is it going to happen again? I really don't want it to. Please."

"It could, but you just have to remember when it happens it's just a stupid Chihuahua. All bark, no bite."

"Oh, no, no, I don't want it to happen again."

"I know. Sometimes we have to go through this stuff. I promise it'll be okay."

There was a moment of silence; the boy's voice became grave. "Dr. Coggler said I might have to take some kind of crazy pills."

"No. Mighty, you don't need any pills or anything like that. You're going to be fine. Dr. Coggler doesn't know shit, okay? Not shit. No way." Walker took a breath and forced a laugh, "You don't need any crazy pills."

"Charlie's on anti-depressants."

"Charlie?"

"Charlie from school. He showed us this yellow pill he's got to take every day, or he'll go nuts and jump off a building or something."

"Jesus, Son. No, you don't need any stupid pill, you're fine; you just had a panic attack. It's normal; hell if you didn't have one, I'd think there was something wrong with you. I promise, it's going to be okay."

"Really?"

"Maybe I should come up there and we can talk in person; this is silly over the phone. I can catch a train, maybe we can rent some surfboards and chat out on the water. Would that be fun?"

"It's November, Dad."

"It's called a wetsuit, Son."

He felt Mighty smile for a moment, but then there was silence on the line, a little too much.

"What about Mom?"

"She'll be fine. Would you like that? We could even bring Minty, if he's not painting flowers in a field or something . . ."

Mighty chuckled then grew quiet.

"Huh, Son, would you like that?"

"Sure, if it's okay with Mom."

Walker was quiet a moment.

"Well, it's okay with me. Don't worry about your mom so much."

"I can't help it," he said quietly.

Walker had the sense that the kid was looking around, making sure she couldn't hear him. He heard him call out, "Mom, Mom!" then nestle under a pillow or something.

"What are you doing? Mighty?"

"I hear her crying a lot. At night."

"Oh."

"Yeah, like she's crying all night. I came in once, but she made me go back to my room."

"What's wrong with her?"

"I don't know."

"Okay, well listen, I'll talk to her; you shouldn't be worrying about your mother."

"I can't help it; I can't help worrying about her."

"Look it's 2 p.m., I'm going to catch a train up there. We're going for lobsters tonight. Would that be fun?"

He heard some voices, and Mighty's changed. "Hey Mom, Dad wants to talk to you. Okay Dad, bye, here she is . . . ." The phone was silent for a while; someone was muffling it.

She said, "Walker?" Then, to the boy, "Okay honey, keep your bother out of the tall grass . . . yes you can go down to the beach, but don't wander off . . . . Walker? Walker, you there?"

"I'm here."

"So what do you think?"

"I'm getting a train, I want to spend some time with him. Talking on the phone isn't the same."

"You sure that's a good idea?"

"Yeah, it's pretty much the only idea. I'll get a room at one of those shit boxes on the beach. I'll call when I get close."

She was silent.

"See you soon, Marika," he said and hung up.

* * *

The train was half-full, a train to Montauk on a Saturday in mid-November. All those party kids with their glow stick necklaces would be back in the city. The trees whizzed by, their awesome colors. Two hours of being nowhere. A place between places. He started to nod off, and then the worst thing happened. An old lady, she must've been 82 or so, sat next to him. He was leaned up against the window, a gray sweatshirt pushed up around his ears for a pillow. He quickly surveyed the train; sure, it had filled up, but it wasn't like she couldn't have picked another seat. There was a person probably in each row, all spread out like civilized people. The lady was dressed up like a Kennedy, in a smart suit, and must've just gone to the hairdresser. She smelled like a tea set, probably had a harangue of dogs with initialled collars tucked away in a brownstone on the Upper East Side, knew how to plant a garden, the names of trees. Damn it. He checked his watch; at least another hour, probably an hour and fifteen. He closed his eyes and tried to go back to sleep.

His elbow must've slipped, and he opened his eyes. She smiled, nodded politely, and looked back down at the crossword puzzle. He peered over her shoulder; she wasn't having much trouble. He thought about his eyes and was grateful, but just for a moment, that he'd kept his eyesight. He could read the clues. Her voice came fast and familiar as if they'd ridden through Asia together.

"*On Earth We Are Briefly Gorgeous*, author."

He didn't know if she was talking to him, but it was certainly out loud.

"Vuong," she said, "But what's his first name? Five spaces."

He was silent. She looked at him, then answered her own question. "Ocean." She was pleased and filled out the spaces. Over the next few minutes, he watched her petite wrinkled hand go to town on the thing, and he had to admit he was impressed. She then suddenly tapped the paper twice with her eraser, folded it, and stuck it in a tote bag that said SHAKESPEARE & CO. She adjusted the bag between her feet, and two bottles clinked rather loudly.

"Sorry," she said. He supposed she was referring to the sound of the bottles.

He shook his head to say it didn't bother him, and looked back out the window.

"Natural wines," she said, and he was forced to say, "Sorry?" because she was talking to him, who else?

"Oh, I was just saying that I'm bringing natural wines; that was the ruckus."

It was amazing that she'd used *ruckus* in this context.

"Oh."

"Have you ever tried natural wine?"

"Uhm, no. I don't know what that is."

"You're lucky, it's like pee in a bottle. Actually, it's like a mouse's, who's eaten lots of stinky cheese, pee in a bottle."

"Doesn't sound great."

"Oh, it's not, but Carla, my grandson's wife, loves it. What would that be, a *granddaughter-in-law*? Would you call it that?"

"Uhm. Yes, probably."

"My *granddaughter-in-law*—my, that sounds ridiculous; anyway she loves it. John, he hates it. My grandson. But that's not surprising, he hates everything."

He nodded and looked out the window. "That happens," he muttered mostly to himself.

"Excuse me," she said sharply, and leaned very close to him with a hand cupped around her ear. "What'd you say?"

"I said *that happens*," he said louder.

"That's what I thought you said; I'm not deaf. These trains are loud."

He nodded again. She reached into her bag, took out one of the bottles and nudged him with her elbow. "Look." There was a naked woman sketched in orange on the label. It said,

Come back K, I love you. She looked at him, confused, and said, "Who is K, and why is this the name of a wine?"

He didn't have an answer.

She shook her head, looking at the bottle. "The fellow at the store said Carla would love it. It's bubbly, light and red. You serve it chilled, apparently. I'm terrified. Here, look . . ." She handed him the wine, and he had no choice but to hold it. The naked lady on the bottle was entwined with the yearning title.

"I don't know much about wine."

"Ha, you remind me of my husband."

"I do?"

"Yes, he's dead but you do."

He wasn't going anywhere, so he said, "Oh, how's that?"

"Well, you look like someone just threw you into that seat. All legs and arms." Walker straightened up a bit as she smirked. "So was Maurice; wherever he sat, he was too big for his seat. You know those big dogs that always sit in their owner's laps, not knowing they're way too big? That was Maurice. With that look on his face, like *I guess I belong here, but maybe I am a little too big, but well, I'm here already, so . . .*" Her tiny shoulders shook for a moment. He looked at her. "That's probably why I sat here," she said. "I'm used to big, silly dogs."

Now he had to exhale a quick laugh; this woman he didn't know had just called him *silly*.

"*Silly*, huh?"

She gave him a playful jab with her eyes. "Oh yes, completely."

She took the bottle, placed it back in her Shakespeare bag, unfolded the crossword puzzle and started attacking it again. There were only a few empty spaces left. He leaned against the glass and watched the tracks speed toward him. When he woke up, she had gotten off, maybe at Southampton or one of those other stops, but she'd left the crossword on the seat. He picked it up and wondered if she'd left it intentionally. Maybe a note or something? Nope. Whether it was intentional or not, it was certainly finished, all in distinct capitals. The train was coming to a halt. He folded the crossword a couple more times, put it in his jacket pocket and walked to the front of the train. He imagined he was arriving in India. He would be greeted by a gaggle of kids with glazy smiles. He'd find a small hotel and lie in bed all night, looking out the window, the millions of people, the stars. What would he think about then? Who?

He got into one of those beaten-up cabs that lurk around train stations and gave the address, but before he got to the little rental just across from the ocean, he asked the driver to stop. He paid and walked the last bit. His little one, Minty, was playing with a fire truck on the small lawn. He stopped and watched him. No one else was around. Minty's blonde hair shined like a burning cup. His gentle one. He had the urge to swoop him up in his arms and run and run and run. He could save him. How he wanted to save him from everything. He was too gentle. But he just stood there. Minty was guiding the fire truck back and forth over a bump in the grass, a stick he'd placed there, and talking to himself; maybe he was making truck sounds.

He doesn't know how long he stood there. The blue arc of sky above him. He lost track of his thoughts. Soon a porch door creaked, and his wife—well, soon to be ex-wife if the lawyers were allowed to proceed—stepped out and stood over Minty. He looked up at her defiantly. He was not coming inside, apparently. Soon, Mighty was next to them also. Mighty sat down with his little brother and held the stick steady as Minty rolled the truck back and forth. She stood over both of them now with a look of mild exasperation. After a while, she went back inside. Mighty watched her as she walked off; Minty kept pushing the truck.

His phone started vibrating; she was calling him. He didn't know why, but he let it ring through. Then, careful to avoid the house, he crossed the street and lay on the ocean-side of a small dune. If he raised his head, he could see the lawn with his kids playing. But he didn't; he lay on his back looking up at the sky which remained cloudless. In front of him, tight-lipped small waves curled toward shore. The fish-colored sea of Montauk. No surfers today, not even a longboard could be carried on this tiny but pristine roller. His phone rang again, and he saw that she was leaving voicemails.

* * *

Minty was a champ at dinner, finished his whole plate, including the coleslaw, and was licking the last drips of dressing from his index finger when he looked up brightly and said, "Lobsters are people too."

Mighty giggled and looked at his father (apparently, these pronouncements from his younger brother were not unusual).

"They are?"

"Yes, red and yummy like my brother," Minty said and leaned over and pretended to chomp Mighty's arm.

After they finished their sundaes (Minty's strawberry, the other two chocolate), he walked behind the boys as they rode their bikes home. They cut each other off on the quiet, almost alien-like quiet, road, shrieking from time to time, skidding this way and that. He dropped them about twenty feet from their door, at which Marika appeared only to shake her head and disappear, which may or may not have been due to the late hour on a school night. He walked back to the motel, showered and got in bed. The bed was springy, tight and cold, but he could hear the ocean, which was more predictive than palliative since it was late fall, and almost midnight.

He usually didn't have trouble falling asleep, but he wanted to be fresh the next morning. He wanted to bring the boys breakfast (bacon-egg-and-cheeses from the deli), a little taste of New York, and take them to school. He hadn't cleared this with Marika, but if he showed up early enough, what was she going to say? Maybe he'd bring her an egg-and-cheese too (she didn't eat bacon). He started the nostalgic ritual that sometimes helped him fall asleep of going back through ex-girlfriends (or crushes), some more serious than others, starting with the first one, a girl in a red-checkered shirt he'd met on a Canadian island when he was eleven and she twelve. Her name was Mimi Silver, and she had not wanted anything to do with him because of that vast eight-month age gap, but on the last night of her August vacation, their families had gone to a dance together; and on the boat ride back, the battered but maintained Riva, cutting through the pulled silk of Muskoka lake water, she'd put her head on his shoulder. He'd never seen her again, but for a full year after, he dreamed he'd open the door of his New York apartment and she'd be standing there in the same red-checkered shirt, having Greyhounded from Buffalo, New York, to make a go of it with him in the big city.

They weren't teenagers yet, but so what? Maybe they'd live in the Museum of Natural History. By the time he got to Bettina, his sophomore year at college—Bettina, who shared his rather common last name, was unliked by her sorority sisters for being a weak team player, as she tended to side with the opposite sex on rather large, current issues; and worse: private, personal ones (she was even rumored to have had an affair with her English professor), but was still unapologetically put-together with her throat-thickening, precociously adult, Fracas perfume—he was asleep.

It was 4:26 a.m. when the fire alarm went off. The slow, spinning wail was almost welcoming. He got up, put on his pants, shoes, T-shirt, threw on his jacket, opened the door and stepped into the hallway, which was twice as loud. The alarm was a circle opening and closing around his head. A few sleepy-eyed, robed patrons muddled around outside as a man in his sixties with short white hair (must've been the manager) curtly assured everybody they'd be back in their rooms soon. He wasn't in a rush. The night hadn't begun to thin, but it would soon. Behind him a few fire trucks and an ambulance pulled up, throwing their lights all over the place. He didn't turn around; he could tell just by looking at the ocean. The flashing lights and the stars were all a mess.

What a ruckus, he thought and allowed himself a short laugh while he reached into his jacket, pulled out the crossword, unfolded it and stared at the letters in their boxes. He still had some questions though: Did the old lady end up liking the wine? Did she think of Maurice before sleep? Who was K, and why did he want her back?

Strange Beds, Strange Houses

She's been asked a difficult question. It's not *Sophie's Choice* or anything, but difficult just the same. She closes the curtains, gets back in bed, pulls the duvet over her head. She decides not to do what she would usually do to relieve stress, sensually distract herself. She wants to feel the rock she's pressed against, the ridges of the argument (the knobs, pockets, holds). Where to place her right foot, left hand, other foot, hand. How to climb out of this hole. She's in that movie where he saws his arm off. That was based on a true story, wasn't it? She could do that; she feels she has to. She has that power, and when you don't use your power, your brain gets sick.

She listens to the lawn mower next door. The smell of cut grass, cliché, affecting. Even if you grew up in New York City, which she did, there were the summers, and you couldn't avoid it, even if you'd never used a lawn mower. She thought of other smells. Gasoline was a favorite. At stations, for sure, but better when it drizzled out of outboards, leaving thin, smashed rainbows on lake water. But the best? The best smell of gasoline was when it pooled in empty boat slips, the red cedar docks soaked with age and petrol. How about that shampoo, which was purported to have beer in it, but, of course, didn't? What was the name? How could she forget the name? How many years, while shopping for other things, she'd scan the line of shampoos, find the amber bottle, pop the top, breathe it in, smell him? That night when she was 15, and they stayed up kissing till 6 a.m. She didn't let him go to third base, really. Their tired hunger finding each other, after saying goodnight for the hundredth time. It was Andrea's house, her mother's bed. The teasing torture for him. He thought the torture was only his. The lawn mower stops.

She surfaces from under the sheets, stares at the ceiling. It's 3 p.m., no one should be under the covers at this hour. Why not? She spreads her arms and legs just to prove she can do whatever she wants. She gets out of bed, walks to the tiny desk, takes out a piece of stationery (not hers), swipes an ant away, uncaps a fountain pen (hers). Her swooping penmanship fills the page:

Muskrat—

There's no way in hell I want to get married. You know that, don't you? So why keep asking? It's not personal, you know if I was made differently or we had to, like if we lived in the Victorian era, I'd marry you in a second. Why do you want this and so suddenly? Have the last eight years been that horrible? And don't tell me kids and all that, because you're aware it's 2022. Nobody gets married. Unless there's something wrong with you. Sure, sure, all those friends of ours, but we were never like them. Are we now? I just don't, I really really really really really really really don't want to, and I hate saying no, because not only do I love you, but I like you. Please don't ruin everything . . .

X

Your Smug Raccoon

She waves the paper around till the ink is dry, folds it and sticks it an envelope. She sits at the desk, staring at it for a while, until she feels an enormous need to sleep. She jumps back into bed and pulls the covers over her.

She's about to enter that downy castle when there's a big knock on the door. The knock is more obnoxious than if he'd kicked it open. He, on the other hand, thinks he's being incredibly considerate to his little sister by knocking, giving her the privacy he by no means owes her.

"Leave me alone, idiot. I'm sleeping!"

Just as loudly as a door can swing, the door slams open, and he fills the frame. He's wearing a flannel shirt and rain boots.

"There's a pond here. Let's fish."

She allows for one eye to pop out from the covers. He's raided a private closet, because neither boots nor shirt is his.

"Where'd you get the duds?"

"Same place I got the fishing rod."

Now she notices a long reflective green rod jammed under his armpit like a thermometer. The line is all messed up, tied to the end with no lure.

"You don't know how to fish."

"The hell I don't."

She can't help but laugh. He looks like a nine-year-old stuffed into the body of a 36-year-old man, ridiculous.

"Where's the pond?"

"Down past that shed and those white trees."

"Birches."

"What?"

"The birches!"

"Why are you yelling?"

"Because I'm trying to sleep and fucking Jack London storms in."

He smiles and sits down on the bed.

"When's he coming?"

She throws off the comforter, revealing she is fully dressed from the waist up, a V-neck powder blue sweater, a gold cross dangling at the tip of the triangle. She wears Brooks Brothers pajama bottoms that must belong to him because they're 80 sizes too big.

"Can I just have one millisecond of privacy?"

She hops up and grabs a bronze Zippo off the desk, snaps it opens and lights a cigarette. She leans on the desk, looking at him. She exhales deeply.

"Don't think you're allowed to smoke here—"

"He's coming for dinner."

"Owners don't usually—"

"Aw, Christ," she drops the cigarette into a glass of water. "Happy?"

"So what are you going to do?" he asks.

"I don't know. I just really don't."

"Do you want my two cents?"

"Absolutely not."

He takes a few casts but the rod scrapes the ceiling; the line gets loose and starts swaying all over the place.

"Stop that!"

"I'm pretty proud of him. Old Walter Scott Ambrose Clark the 157th. Ultimatum. I didn't think he had it in him."

"He does, apparently. It's awful."

"Ah, just come fishing with me. We'll catch him a big old fish for dinner."

"He doesn't eat fish."

"Maybe he can marry it then."

"Funny," she says sarcastically. "Always so funny at the perfect time."

"Okay, so we'll put it in a tank; he can feed it fish food and name it Sally."

"He has an aunt named Sally."

"Oh, Jesus. Then Sally and Sally can honeymoon together."

She puts on her orange fluffy slippers.

"Let's go."

They trudge down to the pond. After she attaches the shiny thingamijig, she rolls up her pajamas, steps into the mud, and casts. He stands next to her pointing out spots he thinks she should aim for.

"Why were you mean about Walter? The 157th? I thought you liked him."

"I do like him. He's great."

"C'mon. What's going on?"

"Nothing."

"Did he ask you to encourage me?"

He doesn't answer. She pulls some gooky grass from the lure hooks. "There's some reason you're not golfing with your bozo friends, standing here in a pond."

"Okay, okay. Just relax. Walter did ask me to put in a word."

She blows the bangs off her forehead and shakes her head. "I can't believe—"

"Don't blow a gasket. That's not what I'm doing."

"Then what are you doing?"

"I'm fishing. We're fishing."

She casts again, angrily, and watches the lure sink. She slowly starts reeling it back as she shakes her head.

"It's so unfair."

"What is?"

"All this talk behind my back. People trying to influence my decisions. I hate decisions. And I hate fishing!"

She throws the rod into the lake and marches up to the house.

When he gets back, she's sitting on the floor in the living room. She has made a small fire. He's carrying the fishing rod and her orange fluffy slippers.

"You knocked a fish out with the rod."

"I'm sorry."

She's poured herself a small whiskey. Wiggling her toes by the fire, she takes a sip, then asks, "Who do you think lives in this haunted house anyway?"

"Probably some 90-year-old debutante nudist." He looks at a dusty bookshelf. "What got into you?"

"I just wanted to get away for a few days. Think things through."

"That worked out spectacularly. Here's a hint: If you want to get away, don't invite your brother, answer your cell every four seconds, then send a dinner invitation to the person you're trying to get away from."

"You know we can never be apart."

"So why don't you just marry him?"

"I don't know."

She leans over and chucks another log on the fire.

"The whole thing is just gross." She takes on this strange baby voice. "Eeeeh, c'mon, let's get married, eeeeh I just want you to marry me, marry me, marry you, are you married, who are you married to; oh, I'm married to blah blah, and blah and blah are married too; eeeeeh, let's go marry each other and do married things."

She leans back, takes another sip and stares at the fire. It's a full five seconds until he bursts out laughing. His laugh's like a barrel going over a waterfall.

"Wow, you hate the fuck out of marriage."

She sighs and shakes her head.

"You've been basically married to him for ten years already."

"I know. It's infuriating."

Her cell starts ringing. She holds it in her lap, her eyes stuck to the flames. The phone stays lit in her palm.

"Are you going to answer that?"

She nods but doesn't move.

"You should really answer. Mr. Magoo's probably knocking on doors with American flags and 'Keep Out' signs."

She taps her phone but it's not ringing anymore.

"Sometimes I just want to smack him with a lamb chop."

Her phone lights up again and she answers while shuffling to the high-backed chair by the window. She sits, gets back up, grabs her cigarettes and lighter on the mantle, and sits again. All the time, she's listening and nodding. She runs the flint wheel under her thumb, making sparks but no light.

"No, Walter, I wouldn't refer to this as *Satan's anus*. It's just the country; god forbid you look at a tree for one second of your life." She shakes her head, her eyes widen. "You just click on the icon that looks like a map and type in the address . . . 23 not 33. . . . My god, you sound like you're 120 years old." She rolls her eyes and sighs. "No, you ARE NOT 120 years old."

Exasperated, she throws her head back, looks at the ceiling. "It doesn't matter if you'd *like* to be. You're 40 going on 400, you prefer that?" She opens her mouth, stares straight ahead, bites her entire lower lip, says, "Fine. See you in one hour and twenty-six minutes." She puts the phone in her lap. "He's the most impossible person I've ever met. Do you know he's coming out with a driver? He never learned to drive a car! The man is forty. Forty! He wants to get married and have kids? What if our baby needed to go the hospital in the middle of the night, and I had a broken leg? Would he give us a piggyback? He can't walk ten paces without an asthma attack. We'd have a better chance with our infant carrying *him*. My god, how did I end up with this man!"

"He made you laugh."

"Yes, but at him. AT him. You're not supposed to marry someone you laugh at."

"Whatever works."

"You're always on his side."

"How's he lost with a driver? Doesn't the driver know how to use GPS?"

"His inadequacy is contagious. I'm losing my fucking mind."

"Simmer down. It's all going to be okay."

She jams the flint wheel; the blue flame shoots up.

"Yeah, that's what everyone says. Always. It's going to be okay."

She snaps the lid shut and looks around the room. "We have no groceries, what are we going to do for dinner?"

"I thought you brought some duck."

She shakes her head. Her lips widen slowly. "I know what we'll do. We'll order pizza from that disgusting little place in town. Walter hates pizza. Also some old garlic bread, he'll probably faint."

"Going to throw pineapple on there too?"

"And lots of Yoohoos. Do they still make those horrible chocolate drinks?"

"Not sure."

"C'mon, you order the pies."

Her brother gets up, stretches, his fingertips grazing the ceiling, then stuffs his big feet into her fluffy slippers.

"Uber."

"What?"

"If your baby was sick and your leg was broken, you'd order an Uber. Or maybe an ambulance."

"What if we lived in the country with no reception or the Himalayas?

"Horse?"

An involuntary laugh, and for a moment, she's seventeen.

"Walter on a horse."

She comes in when he's setting the wine glasses on the dining table. She starts flipping the knives so the edges point toward the fork.

"What are you doing?"

"You know, Walter is no saint."

He pauses, sets the last wine glass down.

"Neither was Mother Teresa, apparently."

"He asked me for a threesome the other day."

His eyes open so wide he loses half his forehead.

"Walter?"

"Yep, he just sits up in bed right when he wakes up, before a good morning or even the shades, and says, 'I think we should have a threesome.'"

"With who?"

"Oh, he didn't get specific. Can you believe it? Walter asking me. I would probably be mad if it weren't so funny."

"Please tell me he wanted a woman as the third."

"Yes, why?"

"Just saying because there are some weird things on those porn channels these days."

"Porn? Walter doesn't know anything about porn."

"What'd you say?"

"Say? I was too busy laughing to say anything. He didn't like that. He stormed off to the shower while I boiled some eggs. Hasn't brought it up since."

The dining room smelled like cats but there was no evidence of them.

"Is that why you're angry?"

"God no!"

She steps into the kitchen, comes back with a pitcher of water.

"I'm more angry about Elizabeth and John. Filling his head. Once you fill a man's head, you can't empty it. It's like trying to wash a cup filled with olive oil. You have to scrub the hell out of it."

"Elizabeth and John?"

"They were over a few nights ago, drunk as hell, and bragging. She basically lets him have a threesome with one of her cute friends a few times a year."

"What!"
She nods, inspecting the table.
"Which cute friend?"
"I don't know, they 'switch it up.'"
"Whoa. Jesus Christ. The lucky bastard."
She looks at him, barks out a crazy laugh.
"GEN Z, baby!"
His phone starts dinging.
"I'll be back in twenty."
When he walks out, she's jamming a candle into its holder on the table.

Half an hour later, he comes back and sets the pizzas in the kitchen. He opens a bottle of red wine (she remembered that), and calls out her name. When she doesn't answer, he calls up the stairs, then walks up. At the door, he listens for a shower but hears nothing. He opens the door, sees the lump of her under the covers.

"What's up, pussycat?"
She doesn't answer, and he gets a creepy feeling.
"Hey." He pokes at what he thinks is a rib.
"Ouch!"
"You're freaking me out. What are you doing in bed?"
"Getting some shut-eye."
It was strange talking to the sheet. She had the duvet jammed up by the headboard but the white cotton sheet was over her, so you couldn't really see where her body parts were.
"I thought we were having dinner."
"I did something pretty bad."

She sits up but keeps the sheet over her head, as if in a teepee.

"Oh."

"I cheated on Walter."

She's so still he feels she's trying to look into his eyes through the sheet.

"Well, I didn't *cheat* cheat, but I pretty much did."

"Okay, can we stop with this nonsense; there's warm pizza downstairs."

"Do you remember Hans Pinkus?"

"Oh my god. Please just stop."

"I bumped into him on Madison. Hadn't seen him in eleven years. He has two kids, three and five. Can you believe that? Two daughters. They are beautiful. His wife works at one of those horrendous magazines."

"Do you want a glass of wine?"

The top of the teepee shakes "no."

"So the next thing I know, we're going to that Irish bar on Lex; and he's ordering a whiskey and I'm having an Aperol Spritz. It was that warm day last week. It felt like the right thing to order. We talked about all the usual things. But I was just remembering when we kissed all night at Andrea's house. We were fifteen! We were pretty naughty; it was a bit more than kissing, but nothing unfixable. His mouth looked the same. Wow, he was the best damn kisser. All I wanted to do was lean over and maul him. Crawl back into Andrea's mom's bed. That's just about the only thing I could think of, as I told him about Walter and everybody. He even asked about you."

"So?"

"So what?"

"Did you *maul* him?"

"Of course not!"

"Then what in heaven's farty ass are we talking about?"

"Well, it just got me thinking, gave me thoughts. Why would I want to kiss the same person for the rest of my life? I'm 29. I should have a few more thrills."

"Great, thrill it up. Can we please, PLEASE go eat?"

"We're waiting for Walter. Go eat a banana or something. Jesus Christ, your stomach."

"You look ridiculous."

"Oh," she whips the sheet off, splattering her hair all over like a French girl. She starts to wipe away the strands.

"So what happened with Hans?"

"We had two drinks, then he had to pick up his daughter."

"Did you get his number or anything? Are you going to see him again?"

"What are you, nuts? I'm with Walter."

He looks at her and laughs that big laugh again.

"You're always laughing at the strangest times."

"My god, you just set a record for the biggest cheating slut in the history of jezebels. Jezzy numero uno! How on earth do you live with yourself?" He adopted a shrill Southern accent, "Woman of ill repute, get thee to a chastity factory!"

"That's not funny."

"Actually, it's hilarious."

"It's not. I had the best kiss of my life when I was fifteen."

"Everyone had the best kiss of their life when they were fifteen because they were fifteen. Get over it..."

"I don't want to get over it. I've been with Walter for eight years. Kissing him is like stepping through a turnstile."

"Fine, go marry Hanky Pinkerballs, but can we just go downstairs. PLEASE!"

"I don't want to marry him." Her voice got small. "I want to marry Walter."

They looked at each other. It was just dark enough to bring out the shiny spots in her eyes. She gestured toward the envelope on the desk. "Bring me that." Sighing heavily, he stood up and brought it over.

"Sit down."

She took the note out of the envelope.

"Okay, you're Walter. Listen to this."

She read him the note. He watched her as she read. A tear glistened in the outer corner of her right eye as she finished: "...your smug raccoon." She put the note back in the envelope, wiped the tear and tore it up.

"Okay, now we're broken up." She threw the pieces on the floor by the bed. "Thank you very much for the time, Walter. It's been great. We should move on." They sat in silence for a while. He put a hand on her cheek, stood up and left the room.

When he got downstairs, he heard the shower turn on. He set the oven to 250 (that was preheat, wasn't it?). He sat at the kitchen counter and poured three glasses of wine.

A Last Stroll Through
Her Favorite City

There was no way, as he walked under the Parisian foliage, the autumn light dripping over him like a thick syrup, he could know that he would die today. But yes, it was true, he'd die by the end of the day; and since there was little he could do about it, if anything, it was probably just as well not to know.

He had left his wife at the rental on rue d'Assas because she was feeling *fluey*, a word he didn't like but she'd used to describe the spasm of congestion that had planted itself behind her nose like a turgid jellyfish, not to mention the flashing aches in her joints and lower back. At first she'd thought it was the monthly gloom, but the intensity made her rethink her initial prognosis and stay in bed that day.

The boys (ages three and six) were playing with their Uzbekistani nanny in the Luxembourg playground across the street. His wife had paid the two-euro-per-child-per-day entrance fee for the week so she could air them out when their levels became savage. For the first time in months, maybe years, he found himself on an aimless walk. He hadn't been to Paris in seven years (his wife had pointed this out; he thought it more like three) when they had spent four months, the first three pleasurably, the last anticipatory, as they waited for the renewal of his then not-wife's American visa. (After the third month, the glow of his wife's favorite city had dimmed, as did the allure of sleeping in rented beds as they pushed up against the invisible bars of the United States immigration system.) But how they loved Paris! She in particular. It made her glow. The midnight dinners in tiny bistros, the warm croissants in the morning, oysters at midday, the long, long walks, making love in the afternoon, the drinks at Bar Hemingway, the classic concerts in small churches, the art shows spilling onto the streets, everybody smoking (even the dogs in cafes seemed to have their own studios), the language perpetually thrown over the shoulder like a cigarette to the wind, the poetry/graffiti on the walls. What was there not to love . . .

He was not thinking of any of that as he walked along rue Bonaparte toward the Seine, but that remembered joy percolated in his blood, making the walk more pleasurable than if he hadn't lived those four months seven years ago. Of course, he had been to Paris other times, and it was those moments that now appeared before him quite randomly. Like sepia prints coming into focus in a darkroom, but instead of chemicals, offering up scents, emotions. One was having dinner with an American painter (she would later become his lover) when he was in his early twenties in her Paris flat, sitting on the floor, amidst some loud Italians, consuming a huge salad, steak and globs of red wine. How she had a pointy Rimbaud face and pretentiously ended all her sentences with a question mark. He had brought his best friend Gregory, a musician (they had randomly bought clogs that day), and she drew sketches of both of them. Vainly, he thought she'd made his face too round, while Gregory's was rendered narrow, artistic. He of course blurted this straight out, and she agreed that his friend was more interesting. Somehow this assured him they'd go to bed together. Other memories invaded: writing at a cafe but having a panic attack and having to leave, barely able to pay as he spat into a napkin; walking home alone at night, just managing some French with a well-dressed homeless guy. Lamp lights. Saint-Sulpice. Falling into bed with his shoes on. The books, the countless books, with their faded, vintage covers.

 He remembered filling up on mini-burgers at L'Atelier and after four years of not smoking, sitting on a bench, turning to a stranger, asking for a cigarette and lighting it. That terror of nicotine slamming his throat giving him a fast buzz as the Vespas sped past him. He noted now, at forty, he was happy he'd quit, and, though he still enjoyed second-hand smoke, had no urge to pick up the vile habit again. He passed one of the cozy brasseries and immediately thought of what he'd have for dinner. He was craving a steak frites and bottle of chilled Brouilly. The thought of that gave him satisfaction. A few teenage girls passed, all wearing crop tops; and he marveled at how little he had in common with anyone under thirty and wondered how he appeared to them. A girl from the take-out counter at a sandwich shop smiled at him; and he smiled back, thinking, *How unlike New York, a woman just smiled at me for no reason.* That felt good, though it was likely kindness, not flirtation. As the Seine appeared before him, he was thinking about tattoos, how everyone seemed to have one. He did not. Also, how most of them now entailed words, sentences; he tried to read them as they passed, but that was impossible. When did everyone get tattoos? His wife didn't have one either; and though he had nothing against tattoos, he was somehow certain that part of the reason he loved his wife (and he did love his wife) was that she was the kind of person who'd never get a tattoo. A horn blast from one of the tourist boats, *bateau-mouche*, stopped him, and he thought, *Well, that's obnoxious*, and remembered a rather conservative childhood friend who once told him, "Horns should be twice as loud inside the car so people think thrice about using them." He thought, *Now, that's a fantastic idea.*

As he walked along the Seine casually looking at the books for sale on the wooden counter tops wrapped in plastic, here's what he was not thinking about: *What happens when we die? Is life governed by chance or fate? Is there a god, and if so, why does he allow such horrors?* Though he wasn't thinking about these things, he had thought of them, and here were his answers in order: *Nothing. Chance. There is no god.*

Now something peculiar happened. As he was casually browsing the books, he came across the familiar cover of a poetry book someone had given to him in his twenties. The book was called *Last Thoughts First* and had a painting of a flower with handwritten script underneath. The background was brown, the flower was light blue and the script was ochre. He picked it up and saw it was inscribed in black fountain ink: *To Jacques, with all my love, Isabelle.* He couldn't help but chuckle. The book was originally in English; and Isabelle Fontana was the French translator, a friend of a friend, who was brought to dinner at his house in New York just after the publication of the book. She'd given him a copy. No one had ever or since given him a book of poems. Since it was put out by a small press, and most likely no more than a thousand copies had been printed, he was quite sure the inscription was from his friend, Isabelle, and it was equally clear that Jacques did not love her back, or he didn't care for the book. He hadn't read it in many years so he flipped through the pages wondering if he'd like it now as much as he did then. Back then he read a lot, had designs to become a writer himself, but had been sucked into business matters after his father's death, and had now overseen the investments of his family office for more than ten years. He knew what terms like Price/Earnings ratio (or PE) meant and what EBITDA stood for. A small pleasure overtook him as he flipped through it. He remembered his own small attempts. Years ago he had found some of his early journals and reread them, thinking it certainly didn't sound like him-himself, but him-somebody-else who was probably more him than him. That's what he had liked about writing, when it was going well, you were a stranger to yourself, but more you than you. At page 49, he stopped at a poem based in Paris. He had particularly liked this one, and Isabelle had told him the author had said it was loosely based on an afternoon spent at the Rodin Museum, very hungover (a usual occurrence for the author at the time), when he was certainly not in love (though this was a love poem) but was aware, he must've been, of longing, mostly from poetry books, and one poem in particular by C.P. Cavafy about looking back at all the extinguished candles of his life, and fearing how few lit ones lay before him. He read the last line, which Isabelle had told him was not directed at any person-person but the idea of a woman, the idea of love, which back then had made it somehow fake to him, though not in a bad way.

A LAST STROLL THROUGH HER FAVORITE CITY

I want to be light and water and hold her in my arms
once more while I am young
and my eyelids hang beneath my lips.

Hang beneath my lips, he repeated, and shook his head. Strange line. He thought about buying the book and sending it to Isabelle with a funny note about Jacques, but decided against it, set it on the counter, thought for a moment whose hands the book would fall into, what stranger would read those exact lines, and if the book would affect him or her the way it had affected him, and then quickly let those thoughts go too, and continued along the Seine.

I suppose this is where the story begins. It was at the corner of rue de Beaune and Quai Voltaire that he saw an ex-girlfriend. A French girl he'd dated for three years in his early thirties. He had walked away choosing to be single rather than marry. She had an erotically Jewish nose and masculine thumbs, and always seemed to have her hand on her hip as if she were at a chic cocktail party (which she often was). Even in movement, when she walked down the street, as she was now, she retained this demeanor of casual elegance, and it seemed impossible she could be unaware of all who noticed her, many turning, as she—partly confused, but mostly ethereal like a ghost from the 1920s trying to find Modigliani's studio or a champagne cocktail—whisped by yet another cafe. But possible it was, as she had no idea of anyone noticing her whatsoever. In short, she was original, and a good, now-known photographer. She had a son, now perhaps ten, named after a famous film director (he didn't remember which one) who walked alongside her, handsomely, more solidly, more actually there, than his mother.

She quickly turned on rue du Bac, and with a last flash of her stylish Mom Jeans, loose silver blouse, and—even now, at what would be 36—her youthful delusion, she was gone. He ran after her in a very un-Parisian, un-casual way, but when he got to the corner, he only saw a portly woman sweeping cigarette butts onto the street. Where had she gone? She had disappeared like a bubble pricked by the past.

Why had he run after her? Not for any lingering romantic affection, but mostly, if he were to be honest (and immodest), because he thought she'd be happy to see him (and he her of course); she'd always been fond of him, regardless of the failed romance, so he thought she'd get a kick out of running into him after what must've been eight years. She'd always called him by his last name, and surely she would've again, and her smile would, as always, be genuine. After they'd broken up, she'd gotten together with a French art dealer; and the one time they'd all run into each other in New York at an opening, the fellow, a handsome congenial sort, had said, "Thank you for breaking up with her, I'm happy to be her second choice," with a rich laugh and no undercurrent of jealousy. He'd been impressed with her new man's confidence and ease, and as she rolled her eyes at the comment, he remembered being happy that she'd found such a *simpatico* partner.

He took a breath and leaned against a lamppost. Once his heartbeat settled, he wondered why he could breezily jog five miles as exercise but any exertion in real life expunged his lungs almost immediately. Was it even her? It must've been. He thought when he got back he'd write her an amusing email (even maybe a little story) about a woman passing an ex-lover without a thought . . . . How we all pass lives that *might've been* without knowing—the spider web of endless lives, loves, vibrating invisibly around us. No—too serious, philosophical; she'd think he'd become sincere. Something more self-deprecating about her being rightfully unaware of his klutzy, eager presence as she sashayed past as if in a foreign movie. He was thirsty and walked into a market, bought one of those awful, ubiquitous (even in Europe) plastic bottles of water, and set on finding a place in the shade to rest and think of nothing at all. He walked across the Pont Royal to Tuileries Garden and looked for a bench, which, since they were in Paris, was not hard to find. He found a quiet one just outside the gate of a children's playground. He thought this would be a relaxing spot. Children, who'd been virtually invisible to him, had become tolerable, almost interesting, after having his own. Or at least watching the way parents interacted with their children, how they parented, had become interesting; their levels of impatience and degrees of punishment as points of comparison to his own style. It was a language he understood and thus found soothingly familiar (especially as an observer, perhaps only as an observer). Content, he sat and sipped the cool water. He watched the kids run and scream and swing and play . . . the quiet ones, the screamers, the observers and loners, the boisterous little groups popping with shrieks and imagination, until suddenly, he saw his eldest with his straw-colored bowl haircut run past the swings (he sometimes had an unusual sideways run) and duck inside a wooden boat. *Wow, she brought them all this way to a new park. What a great nanny*, he thought as he often had about her. *We're so lucky.* He looked around; she must be close by, probably playing with the younger one. But he couldn't see her. He scanned the playground for the little one, who was hard to miss for he was very tall for his age and screamingly blond. Nowhere. He thought, *Pretty irresponsible leaving the eldest alone.* He was a mature six, but still six the same, and he didn't speak French. He got up, unlatched the gate, stepped into the playground and ducked underneath the boat but his son wasn't there. Where is he? He started to question whether it was his son, or had he imagined it? No, it was him, the kid was even wearing the T-shirt with the rainbow and "All Good" printed on the back in bubbly script. He couldn't have imagined that. Strange. He took another look under the boat, then peered around. He looked at each kid. No. No. No. No. The sun, high and bright, wasn't helping. He sat down on another bench, now inside the playground, and looked around, hoping one of them would pop out from a covered slide or an underground ladder, but nothing. His throat was dry again. He took the bottle out of his jacket and swallowed the last of it. The water was warm.

What an unusual day this is becoming, he thought, and wondered if he too didn't feel *fluey*. He felt his forehead with his palm (no fever), and took his pulse, though he didn't know how, was more just checking if his heart was beating fast, and it was, but what did that mean anyway? Wouldn't anyone's heart beat fast if their son had appeared and disappeared in a strange park just like that? He was not *fluey*. He didn't dislike, but hated that word. He took a last look around and even called out the name of his eldest, then youngest, then nanny. He knew he looked ridiculous. Alarmed, some parents looked up and followed his gaze in a purely symbolic gesture of help. He opened the gate and walked toward home.

He had gone about six blocks down the rue de Rivoli when he saw his father walking toward him. He was wearing a dark blue suit and carrying an old-fashioned, tan briefcase, the bulky square kind with the gold latches. He stopped and stared. As he walked by he could barely say the word *Dad?* But his father didn't look up, just kept walking. He only made out the kerosene blue of his eyes as he passed. He groped his way down a side street and sat on a step. Everything was bending above him, the mansard roofs leaning toward each other, almost liquefying. His heart was certainly pumping now, and he thought he might be having a panic attack. One of those hysterical episodes of his twenties when he'd need three drinks to steady him. When he next looked down, he was reading the poetry book, but as he tried to close the book, the pages crumbled like sand to his feet. He got up and ran, knowing, or at least very strongly feeling, that the only way he could get through this was to get home to his wife. She would pour him a glass of Japanese whisky and put him to bed. He'd lie right next to her, hold her tight. This kind of stuff can't happen when you're holding your wife. Now he was sprinting, hoping the physical exertion would overtake his mental collapse—or whatever the hell was happening—and distract him enough to get him home. An old French couple stopped and stared as he ran; a woman yanked her Yorkie out of his path. He didn't want to imagine the frightful look of terror that must've been on his face. He got to the Seine and was breaking a sweat when it overtook him; he knew he wouldn't make the apartment. It might've been the sky opening up that sunk him, no crowded buildings to protect him, but instinctually and for what he perceived as pure survival, he took a hard left down the steps, jumping three at a time, toward the river. He sat on the dirty cement close to the water, took off his shoes and rubbed his feet with both hands. He did this to remind himself that he was still here. That he was a human being. That he was okay. He sat there a long time.

It was unclear how long he'd been out, but it must've been a while, because the colors had changed. The heavy magic gray of late afternoon had coated the buildings on the other side of the river. He got up, collected his shoes, felt dizzy, stepped back from the embankment and sat on yet another bench. He pulled on his shoes and leaned back, looking at the water, which was sparkling a little now. The animal terror had left him, and he almost smiled at the ludicrous day. He thought, *I'll sit here just a while and then walk home.* He closed his eyes and took a deep breath, happy to be back in his body.

When he opened them, he began to make out a little raft toward the center of the river, bobbing with the current as if anchored. It was one of those bamboo ones with the shoots tied at their ends by coarse rope. Something he imagined Huck Finn would float down a river on. When he looked closer, he saw there was a girl of eight or nine sitting on it. She had on a funny, frayed sun hat and was smiling. She was somehow familiar to him and had seemed to have shaken off all of life. She was fresh, pure, but not because she was a girl on a raft in the middle of Paris, but for some other reason. He wasn't sure. She uncapped some ChapStick and applied it. After she finished, she popped her lips and opened her mouth. He could see her white teeth. He thought of his wife. As a child. He thought she would've been like the girl in the hat. Bobbing. On a raft. With a hat that was more tear and cloth than hat.

He stood up and walked toward her but didn't call out. He wanted to surprise her.

Around this time, his wife had gotten out of bed and fixed herself an omelet. The boys were still playing in the Luxembourg playground but would be coming home soon. She felt well enough to open a bottle of chilled Brouilly. *Why not*, she thought, this was still her favorite city.

When they found him, he was seated upright, hands folded in his lap, an untouched newspaper by his side. Only the position of his head gave it away. The sun was low now. Some red and yellowish light falling over the Seine in bursts like rain showers. Under different circumstances, perhaps any, he would've agreed with her about Paris.

Aren't You Glad I Called?

She was a hopeless listener, and he was trying to tell her that, "If you never listen, you're never going to learn anything." He looked over at his wife for help. "I mean, isn't the word for wisdom in Sumerian *ear?"*

She wasn't having it.

"Really, John? You're bringing the Sumerians into this?"

She switched into the HOV, just hitting 76 miles an hour on I-495.

"Yes, I am. So anyway, sweetie, it's very important to listen, especially to Daddy and Mommy."

He looked back at her. Josephine was buckled into the middle of the back seat so she could look out the front. She was six.

"Are the Sumernans Egyptians?"

John looked at Linda, then back at Josephine, clearly impressed, "No, sweetheart. They are older than the Egyptians, but that's very close."

"Are they from Mesopopotamus?"

"Yes! From Mesopotamia. That's great Jo, how'd you know that?"

She was flying her unicorn around like a rocket ship.

"We study old people at school."

John's face was lit up. "That's great. Old people know stuff." He looked at his wife, who was biting her lip at some slowpoke in the HOV. "I love this," he lowered his voice, "*fricking* school." They'd just passed Exit 66 and there was no traffic except for the grandma in front of them.

"Why the hell—" Linda caught herself, "Sorry, honey, why the *who* would you get in the fast lane and go 56 miles an hour. I mean. I mean." She banged the steering wheel twice with her left palm. "Who does that?" She looked at John to see if he thought she was overreacting. He raised a palm and lowered his chin. It's true the driver was going obnoxiously slow, and now Linda would have to illegally cross the wide double-line to get back on the normal highway.

"What's wrong with people?" she said.

"Okay, baby."

"Don't *okay* me, I hate it when you do that."

John took a breath and said nothing. Anything would set her off now. She was looking for it.

"So Jo, what's the deal with this kid Billy?"

"Billy's my friend. He likes bananas."

"Oh does he?"

"Yes, with him everything's about bananas. He says, 'Bananas, bananas, bananas. That's bananas.' He says it all the time!"

"Sounds like an interesting chap."

"No, he's not a chap, he's a boy. His name is Billy."

"Yes, I know, I just asked you about him."

Linda had had enough and crossed the double-line and was now passing the grandma who was not a grandma at all but a guy with a big nose wearing a Houston Astros hat. She stared at him as she passed.

"Asshole," she muttered.

"Oooooh mommy said a bad word. Mommy said the butt word."

"How'd you hear that, you little bat?"

"I'm not a butt! You said the bad word, not me." Josephine crossed her arms and looked down. John stepped in. "Your mother said *bat*—you know, the squeaky animal with the wings that flies around at night on Halloween. They have impeccable hearing. Mommy would never call you a butt."

"Well, I'm not speaking to her."

"Oh, Jo," he said as Linda shrugged.

"Hmph," said Josephine and looked as far away as possible. Josephine was silent for a whole three minutes.

"How many days is Halloween?"

"We had Halloween two weeks ago."

"How many days until Halloween again?"

"Okay, that's a great question. Well, you know it takes 365 days for the earth to go around the sun. You remember that song?"

"Yes."

"Well, how many days in a week?"

"Seven."

"So how many days in two weeks?"

"Please stop," Linda said.

He looked at her. "Why?" Then continued, "Do you know, Jo, if there are seven days in one week, how many in two?"

Josephine stared into the unicorn's eyes.

"Jo, you listening?"

She didn't answer.

"Will you leave her alone?"

"We're just talking."

Linda exhaled and shook her head. He looked back at Josephine.

"What's seven plus seven?"

"14."

"Yes, that's great honey! Now this is a hard one, if you take away 14 days from 365 days, how—"

"I can't take this," Linda said, blinking hard twice, swerving back into the fast lane, making sure not to look at John, the last of the yellow leaves on either side of the highway blurring, beaten, and a bit red at their edges.

It had been somewhere in Wyoming as they swooped around a large mountain turn, a populous of solitary crags streaked with rivers of snow in the afternoon light to the north, that she had spat at him. She was 21, he was 20, and they were on their way to Ketchikan, Alaska to work in a cannery. They'd been fighting about something, and she in anger (never done it before or since) had spat right into his cheek, and then, god knows where this had come from, laughed. A large mocking one, a laugh you hear in schoolyards that kids remember, accompanied by a pointing finger. Adrian had a fine, almost feminine profile with a long nose; and when the spit landed, he raised his right hand, reflexively, then stopped himself, held the spit to his cheek, and kept driving. For years, she'd wished he'd hauled off and slapped her. He was studying Chemistry at Columbia and she Geology, and they'd fallen in love at the Riverside Tennis Courts, him playing, her watching. He had divisible eyes the color of pennies with less of the shine, a photographic memory, and a shirt that was always half-unbuttoned. With his long hair and flannel shirts, she thought he looked more grunge guitarist than chemist, but sometimes when he stared at her, an analytical coolness overtook him, which made her feel he was older than she was, and might be more chemist than she thought.

When they'd gotten to the cannery, the fishermen were on strike, so they slept in a place called Tent City, which was filled with a mix of teenage, pre-nostalgic hippies and lumberjacky, rougher types, who came for the long hours, the overtime. The kids talked Tom Robbins books; the men scoffed. They spent three days with their tent on a pallet so they didn't get swallowed by the mud, the constant rain. He was silent, mostly; she flirted. The guys were happy to have a brushed, natural brunette with direct thoughts and eyes; she even knew French.

She enjoyed nudging Adrian with the flirting, just enough needling, hopefully, she thought, to force him to admit he was jealous, but he just watched her coolly, rolling bummed Drum cigarettes, a little off to the side, while she asked penetrating questions to guys about who they were, *truly*, and what they wanted in life, *really*, why they were with their girlfriends if they didn't love them, *hopelessly*, why they hated their fathers, *unremittingly*. And finally, her advice would be doled out with a little bit of judgment (and perhaps more satisfaction at her own insight) from the somewhat insurmountable height of a woman who knew she was desired and faced no competition. Of course, he was ignored. No one wanted the boyfriend around, even when he told them about an expedition he went on the previous summer to prove the coelacanth off the

Comoros Islands could survive recompression because it didn't have a gallbladder. He had held one in his hands, the fucking dinosaur fish! No one gave a crap. Everyone looked at him as if he was misplaced, something not uncommon for him in any environment; and later that evening, in the dimming, dirty light, she said, "Why are you acting so strange?" It was true, he was. Although he looked like a hippie, he wasn't into anything communal, as much as he would've liked to have been, though he wasn't sure about that—being part of anything *groupy* made him feel somewhat false, as if he were standing on wormy legs. When she asked him again, a few nights later, when they finally got a job and a bed in the bunkhouse, after making love on top of the fitted sheet that would not stay fitted, he said, "I don't know, I was just telling them about the damn fish."

He liked the work. She complained, though it was her idea. Like some other girls he knew, but fewer than you'd think, she liked to set up false tests to prove she wasn't who she really was. The whole no-money, drive-to-Alaska, cannery-thing was poised as a rebuke to her Upper-East-Side upbringing and meant to be a gesture toward a life of rebellion which would never come. He worked the slime line where you'd scoop out the salmon's blood with a thick, squat spoon and yank off its heart over a watery table with nozzles for rinsing, before placing the Koho or Sockeye on the chute. Some of the kids would pop the hearts in their mouths, swallow them without chewing. Two-hour intervals, a fifteen-minute break, thirty minutes for lunch and dinner. Sixteen-to-eighteen-hour days. She was pretty and drowsy, didn't take the extra hours. The foreman let her handle the eggs. His name was Kevin and he wore high yellow boots, had long perfectly combed wavy hair that was usually pulled in a tight pony tail and eyes that seemed to be yanked from Jesus of Nazareth's (or at least the idea of his) skull. A piercing finality to them that could kill or heal. He rode a Harley up from Albion, Michigan for the season and could most likely be one scary dude, which was handy when an ex-employee, a loping bear of a man with wispy brown hair who had been fired and was bi-polar as hell, showed back up one day with an eight-inch Bowie knife and wandered up and down the bunkhouse humming *Mary Had A Little Lamb*. Kevin ran him out of there pretty hard. But even he, the bi-polar bear-guy, Jersey was his name, had wanted to speak to Linda and came back that night, knocked at her window, and, after an hour of conversation about god knows what, had called her *sister*.

Adrian worked as much as he could; it was methodical, repetitive, the same thing over and over, like being crazy, but not.

On one of those nights, a young couple from another cannery had drunk a lot and gotten into a screaming fight right in front of the bunkhouse. They had woken up most of the workers and then disappeared. Adrian had been called into the office the next morning because everyone had assumed it was him and Linda. This was embarrassing for Adrian, who would never cause a scene like that. When Adrian told him they'd been asleep, Kevin fixed him with those eyes and said, "You're a great worker; I don't want to fire you, so sort it out." He'd assumed Adrian was lying, which was both embarrassing and insulting; he couldn't decide which bothered him more. When he went back and told Linda that they'd been accused of fighting, waking up the whole place, she just looked at him strangely. She didn't seem to care at all.

In their few hours off, they'd go to the dump and watch the black bears, sometimes drinking whiskey from a flask. If they looked up, they'd see bald eagles, circling, gliding, cutting through the light rain as if it were easy, and the world was a warm, brown place. Three years is how long they lasted. After they broke up, she didn't remember how many years later, he married a marine biologist with a tolerance for pain and moved to Rajasthan. They'd kept in touch vaguely, a yearly email on birthdays, a random hello, pictures of Josephine after she married John (he never had kids, she didn't think).

"Can you guys please be quiet just for one second, please?" she said, lowering her forehead to the steering wheel. John looked at her as they whizzed by cars on the right.

"Do you want me to drive?" John said, but he knew she'd say no.

She shook her head, looked in the rearview mirror, then accelerated after a flatbed with lightning bolts on its flaps.

No one said anything till Exit 70, and AC/DC's "Back in Black" came on.

Josephine sat up. "Is that Rock High School?"

"No, that's the Ramones. This is AC/DC," John said.

"Billy likes Rock High School."

"He does, huh?"

"It's his favorite. Sometimes Miss Andrea plays it at clean-up."

"Is he your boyfriend?"

"Eeeeeewww gross."

Linda kept looking forward but managed to say, "That is gross."

"Billy's my husband, not my boyfriend. Boyfriends are grosssssssssssss."

John smiled. "Your husband? When did you get married?"

"We get married every day at lunchtime."

"Every day?"

"Gemima can't sit with us. She's always giving Billy candy but we say no no no no."

"Well, you should be nice to Gemima, she's sharing. That sounds nice."

"She's only sharing with Billy. That's not sharing. She's trying to team up on me."

Linda muttered, "Gemima sounds like a bitch."

John smiled involuntarily.

Josephine was getting worked up. "I really want to punch her in the face."

"Now, Jo," John said, "We don't hit people, we use our words."

Linda whispered just below kid-hearing level, in a '40s wise-guy accent, "Words? Sometimes you gotta cut a bitch."

John lost it; Linda didn't flinch.

Josephine said, "What's so funny, daddy?"

He could barely respond as he was doubled over, but managed, "It's just your mother; your mom is bananas."

"Bananas," Josephine said. "Bananas, bananas, bananas."

There'd been a call though, six weeks ago. How many years since they spoke on the phone? It was a Saturday, and John had taken Josephine to a birthday party at a place in Tribeca where kids roll around on mats, jump on trampolines, throw cushions, the usual kindergarten chaos. It was his turn and she'd stayed home, had a late breakfast, was sitting in bed enjoying the peace of October light spilling onto their reclaimed wood plank floor when her cell rang. She felt a warm pleasure when his name popped up, the same number he had twenty years ago, knowing she had time to talk. He'd laughed when she picked up instead of saying hello as if they'd just swallowed their past two minutes ago in their coffee. He told her how he'd moved back and was "taking some time" and staying with his parents; his father was old, sick. His voice was like a kettle, shiny, volatile, and asked something of her, but she didn't know what. He talked about how strange it was to be back, sleeping in his "tiny fucking bed," and she was thinking of a night in Whitefish, Montana. They'd gone there after the cannery for a few weeks to visit friends who'd rented a small house. Instead of washing their clothes, they'd chucked them, still in their clear plastic bags. The stink of the dead fish wouldn't come out. It was the second night, and they were in one of those Moose-y bars with carved-up picnic tables, drinking whiskey. It was his birthday, and she'd drunk too much, often the case back then. They'd been laughing over a joke Katrina, one of the biologists, had made, and Linda thought it'd be funny to slap him. Maybe she was showing off. When he didn't react, she slapped him again and then a third time, this one very hard, harder than ever before, and he'd looked at her for a moment and slapped her back. Not hard, but solid enough. Very calmly, he'd said, "Don't slap me." Later she announced that since it was his birthday, he could do whatever he wanted to her that night; that was her gift, he could have her body any way he'd like. "Whatever you want!" she shouted twice. *How embarrassing*, she thought now; and when they'd gone out the back door of the bar, she pulling him by the hand under the brassy light of the small parking lot, and dim, vaporous stars, she'd offered herself, right there in the lot, but she could tell he'd had enough of her buzz that night. Her outbursts, her violence. They'd gone to sleep later silently, their backs barely touching.

Now his talk had gone strange as she listened, pushed back against her headboard, a pillow in her lap, which she gathered in her arms, from time to time. He was talking about the possibility of disgrace. She remembered that phrase and still didn't know exactly what it meant, and why he was saying it. "You have to be aware of it, always, Linda," he said. "The possibility of disgrace." She was just listening now, as if his voice were a musical instrument sounding from a dark forgotten part of the body, maybe behind the knee, or another lonely place. He had a soft, carrying voice that could reassure you, even knowing if you scraped a bit, it was a car skidding off a bridge. He told her how if you lay across a lake in December, your whole body like a sheet of lightning, in the most northern part of India, you could breathe in god's fingers. She didn't answer, because how would she know? And then he was talking about retribution, and a certain uncanned, yellow light. If you listened very carefully, it sounded almost relaxing, almost like music.

Years after they broke up, she was at a party in Dumbo, just married to John, at an apartment with a view of the Manhattan and Brooklyn Bridges, where she met another woman who'd dated him. There had been crossover. How did he come up? She couldn't remember, but she was shocked to hear that they'd carried out a brief affair while they'd been dating. Or she'd been the one having the affair with him. They couldn't tell. The two women, while sticking chunks of Swiss cheese and chorizo with toothpicks, tried to piece it together. Both marveled he'd do such a thing. She was an English girl, bony, chic, with breasts that pointed sideways under a silk blouse. "Can you believe it?" she said. "Adrian Adams. Can you fucking believe it?" He hadn't kept in touch with her, and the English girl didn't know he was married and living in northern India. Linda thought about mentioning it now, on the phone, his transgression, but his language was a wiry hum. He was high up there. She had let him go too long, too far; meaning had become musical death at that distance. She knew she wouldn't tell John about the call when he came back with Josephine probably holding a gift bag, a rose balloon tied to her wrist. She was a Scorpio that way, and her usual gear was silence, secrecy; as if something shared was in part stolen. After a while, she realized she was listening to nothing. His voice had stopped; she couldn't even hear him breathe. Suddenly, Adrian laughed. "Aren't you glad I called?"

It was Adrian's sister who sent her the notice. The memorial was going to be in a small red church by the sea in Southampton, NY. He'd grown up there.

Linda couldn't have told you why. Adrian couldn't have told you why. No one really knows why. Whether the first malignant skip of a cell. Or urge, thought, that gathers power and ends in a fist, in the dirt. No one. *Cause of, reason for,* don't tell us anything. So many things pile up on us. You can never know. No matter who tells you what. So many things.

They were squeezing into the one-lane road and passing the Chris Craft shop with several boats resting in front on unhitched trailers like toys going down a sink when Josephine said, "Mommy's sad."

John looked at Linda. Linda looked straight ahead. Her Palladian forehead, the Greek proportionality of her profile. He had never seen someone more strong, more knowing, more beautiful. No, that wasn't it; it had nothing to do with him. There simply wasn't anyone more strong, more knowing, more beautiful. She was not circumstantial. They were not circumstantial. John turned and watched Josephine for a while, thought of saying something, then settled back in his seat.

"Don't be sad, Mommy."

Josephine picked up her unicorn and started flying it around like a rocket ship again.

"All the Mesopopotamans are dead too."

The Reunion

I first met him at a college away-football game somewhere in dreary Massachusetts. God knows why I was there because I don't care about football, and school spirit induces a vague, lingering nausea in my larynx. But I'd gone with a friend from the faculty who'd been swallowed by the scarfed masses; and after the game, slightly buzzed, I found myself wandering the parking lot enjoying the colors of the fallen leaves and smashed beer cups when a kid from my creative writing class called my name. It's kind of hilarious to refer to her as a *kid* considering everything that came after, but at that point, that's what she was: a kid.

I almost didn't take the ride because I saw he was chafed she'd called my name. It was starting to rain, and he had his arms purposely dead at their sides and his chin yanked up so I could see his Adam's apple—a childish gesture of annoyance that he probably would've covered up if he hadn't had a few beers. I thought about lying and saying I had a ride, but it was obvious I didn't; and that lie would've matched his childish gesture, and after all, what did I care if her boyfriend was upset. He was one of my students too, but only in my larger English

THE REUNION

Lit class, whereas she took my creative writing one as well (I only taught two). As I opened the backdoor to his used Volvo, I had a thought (later proved correct): He was only taking the class to be closer to her. It was fleeting, inconsequential, but I recall it. A couple other kids were squeezed in the back, but I remember their faces only as blurry representations of every other student at school. At that point, none of this was my business, so I zoned out as we headed pretty fast down I-91.

I probably would've forgotten the whole car ride except there was an event I'd remember even if what happened in the future didn't happen. As I said, he was driving fast. Maybe 85 or 95, which didn't bother me. I like to drive fast. Hell, I prefer it. He had had a few beers but wasn't drunk. No big deal, I drive liquored up all the time as long as I'm not smashed. Might've been the booze, or maybe he was always chatty outside class, but he was spouting some libertarian crap that these preppy rich kids always peddle, all about pulling themselves up by their own bootstraps, when the whole world's been handed to them, even this piece of shit Volvo. Getting into politics with teenagers wasn't my thing (even though I wasn't that much older, having attended the same college on scholarship seven years earlier), but I remember how ridiculous he was. He struck me as one of those kids who had money, the key to freedom, but would lock himself in a cage of misery by choosing to do something he didn't want to do, just to prove he was doing it on his own. And be proud of it. But later would become bitter and lash out because he knew he'd fucked himself.

One of the kids in the back made a comment about him running for office; and I don't remember his reaction, but thought, at the time, that was something he imagined in his future. I don't know why, but I felt it to be true. Maybe because there was no comment from his girlfriend. Maybe it was something they'd discussed, that was understood. Suddenly she said, "Babe, slow down, I think there's a cop up there." Now, this is the moment I would've remembered anyway. Instead of slowing down, he looked at her condescendingly and held the look for a dangerously long time while accelerating. In a flash, I saw who he was, why I'd never vote for him. I saw why he did it. Her mentioning the cop insulted him, told him, *I'm aware of something you're not; I'm pointing out a potential danger that you're not aware of, but you should be because you're speeding. Buzzed. And could get in trouble.* All logical, helpful. Almost anybody would slow down, say thanks. But to him it was different. Her warning said: *I, your girlfriend, who you're supposed to protect, am actually protecting you. Protecting all of us from something silly, even irresponsible, that you're doing.* (Or, *Hey, dumbass, pay attention.*) It challenged his masculinity, pricked his ego. And his condescending look to her said, *Baby, that's not a cop; sit tight, I got this. I'm in control.* It was an embarrassing glimpse into male fragility; also a little dangerous because he was tipsy and speeding without watching the road just to prove his point. Minutes later when he was pulled over, to her credit, she didn't gloat. Luckily, he wasn't breathalyzed; I just remember the tip of his right ear turning red as he handed over his license and registration, in what I hoped was a pinch of shame.

* * *

Embarrassment the next day in class? Not at all; if anything, he paid less attention. Every once in a while, I'd glimpse him scribbling in his notebook; I'm certain nothing to do with our discussion. She, on the other hand, was more awake, alert. More confident in her comments. And out of the 35 kids in class, she probably did 20 percent of the talking that day. She had a crooked nose and eyes that changed colors with her sweaters. But all in all, nothing much had changed. Not until after winter break. It was the poem really that started this.

In my creative writing class, each student had to turn in a weekly poem; and every class, two students would distribute copies of their poem and read them, opening up their work to a class critique. The writing was usually bad but sometimes lively and would take us in a lot of directions; unfortunately, most of it dissolving into some form of therapy, which was awkward and gooey, but never totally boring. In addition, we'd read a new book of poems each week. Her work was above average, and she was sailing toward a safe B+, having advanced from imitation into finding traces of her own voice. She knocked on my office door, and I was surprised to see her, because no one took advantage of daily hours. She was supposed to read her poem the next day and wanted to ask a question. She was standing, so I gestured to the chair. She unfolded a piece of paper and squirmed in her seat.

"I don't know if I should read this to the class."

She wore funky, green reading glasses; it was hard to see her eyes. No student had checked with me before, so I was curious as I took the poem and read it. I wish I had it here, but I don't have a copy and doubt she does either. I don't remember any lines or phrases, but I do recall what it was about. It was about making love to her boyfriend but only being able to reach orgasm if she imagined other people watching. And the strange guilt she felt because she allowed him to believe that he was giving her immense pleasure when in fact she was responsible for her own, and he was just doing the hard rowing while she directed the boat toward the grand prize, and how she wished he'd direct it but didn't think he knew how, and if he was perhaps the wrong man for her, because the right one would know. This all took place while watching him sip orange juice in the morning reading *The New York Times*.

"What's the question?"

She tilted her head and stared at me thoughtfully.

"What would you think if someone wrote this about you?"

"I'd think it was honest."

She nodded. She was struggling, but it wasn't emotional. It was intellectual.

"Do you have to tell the truth, even if you know it'll hurt someone?"

I looked at her. She continued, "In art, I mean."

"The reader can feel when you're lying, so if you're going to, I wouldn't bother."

"Would you find this insulting as a man?"

I didn't like the way she kept bringing me personally into this.

"Me? No, but I'm not him." I regretted saying this, because it was a dig at her boyfriend. When I look back, I wonder if I was flirting with her, or trying to place myself above him. I think I might've been though I was unaware at the time. She seemed to get it, though. She smiled and looked down.

"I think he'd mind."

She left soon after saying that. But I had an uneasy feeling in my stomach that I'd done something wrong. That we'd colluded against him, and I shouldn't have. The next day when she distributed her poem, it was about a painting by Frida Kahlo in which she's split down the middle. I don't remember much about that one.

Over the next few months she'd drop poems at my office, usually when I wasn't there. Ones she wouldn't share with the class but were bolder, sexual. I don't know if they were poems, but they were blaringly confessional and honest. They soon began to explore her guilt about showing me this writing and not her boyfriend. And one was a direct confession that she'd masturbated while imagining making love to me. I admit, I got a little swept up in this . . . . Maybe it was an ego trip, but the air started to get, let's say, a little more *Brazilian*, more humid; she lingered after I read them, even though she was pure American boniness; and any carnality I imagined existing within her, was due to her acute mind, not her physicality. But of course, this was ridiculous, non-professional, definitely grounds for firing; most likely, even entertaining these poems without seeking advice from the higher-ups would warrant dismissal. But I didn't. I did, however, think I should put an end to it, and emailed her to come by my office with the idea of letting her know.

When she showed up, the first thing I noticed was she was wearing loafers; and I remember thinking, *I didn't know they made loafers for women.* The second was that her black-knit sweater made her eyes brighter and deeper, like polychromatic green flowers; and finally, that those eyes looked right into mine with no trace of embarrassment about all the gorgeously erotic poetry, some involving me, she'd been dropping at my office.

Look, I tried.
I swear.
I tried.

An hour or so later, she wordlessly walked out, with a funny look over her shoulder of dominance, apology and flirtation. It was a damn funny look.

Okay, let's examine this.

Morally. Was it wrong for a 27-year-old teacher to have sex with his 20-year-old student? Probably. I mean, he'd definitely be fired from his job, but that doesn't mean much nowadays in terms of morality. She had a boyfriend. Okay, that's kind of her moral lapse, isn't it? I would argue it wasn't wrong, and I think when you see what came later you'll agree.

Professionally. Stupid. Vastly stupid. Though the job came pretty easily, and it wouldn't break my heart to lose it.

Personally. Satisfying. And then some.

The affair blossomed. It started with more emails, and soon she was sneaking over to my place most days, and even was able to spend the night from time to time when her boyfriend would take off on a guys weekend, which usually involved puking and playing golf. There was talk of books and reading of poems, and home-cooked dinners and cheap but thoughtful bottles of wine. And yes, there was even talk of love. She mentioned it first, and I didn't disagree. It was all new, peculiar, lovely.

Of course, there was her boyfriend. Invariably, he came up. As far as young couples go, they were unusual. They'd gotten together at boarding school junior year, purposely applied to the same colleges, and stayed together for four years, an act of hopeful insanity for kids that age. They both came from distinct but identical towns in Connecticut and had non-divorced parents. Their parents could belong to the same country clubs, and probably voted similarly in every election. It was all weirdly congenial. At times, when she slept, looking at her pale, toned arm draped over my chest, I wondered why she was doing this. There was nothing in her history that would foretell her hopping in bed with her creative writing teacher and cheating on her boyfriend in an almost prescribed, domestic way. I mean, this was not the 1960s; this was decidedly uncool, considered almost criminal on most college campuses. But still there was nothing of the adventurer, the thrill-seeker in how she cooked her mother's favorite dishes for me: shepherd's pie, vegetarian lasagna, beef bourguignon; and brought leftovers in pink Tupperware from her monthly visits home.

I'm not sure why I continued the affair. I could've ended it any time, especially when the breathless aspect dissipated after a few months. Why didn't I? I guess I liked her; it was fun, deep and real to me. I'm sure I enjoyed the horribleness of it too. How it would raise eyebrows if anyone knew. It seemed unthinkably rebellious in its *fuck you* to conventional college ethos. I just don't know.

Back to the boyfriend, and maybe the oddest aspect of our affair: She didn't break up with him but continued living out their relationship as if I didn't exist. Us blissful, he blissfully ignorant. In other words, even though she'd professed deep feelings for me, she didn't consider breaking up with him. It was as if I were a separate life, and that was fine. Both lives could exist without devouring the other. I'd be talking about Walker Percy's *The Moviegoer*, and they'd be sitting side by side, even exchanging a laugh, a tender look. What rights did I have on her? I was strangely not jealous, but maybe I should've been. Surely, I never asked her to break up with him. Sometimes I'd imagine them making love and feel sick to my stomach, but it seemed so unreal it was hard to dwell on. Other moments, I'd watch her writing in her staticky black notebook or reading a book and imagine what it was like for her to be carrying on two full relationships. Then I'd vacillate between thinking her spoiled or ragingly mature; I couldn't decide which.

Our relationship continued into the summer, when she'd sneak away between her vacation time with her family in Maine and her weekends with him in Nantucket. We even took a few sweaty trips to New York to get lost in all that. Whiskey, music, East Village, night. But in the fall, back at school, we picked up right where we left off until a Sunday in late October, when she walked into my kitchen (she had keys at this point), dropped her books on the table and announced she'd told him everything.

* * *

OK.
Reality.

Being revealed in an affair shines a light on what an asshole you've been. You can't hide in the blanket of sensuality, the forgetful-making gaze of your lover or the beef fucking bourguignon. You have to face that your actions hurt someone gravely. A real walking-around-living person with their own insecurities and wants. And that you've placed your wants over being truthful, over their feelings. That's fine, but you should be an adult. Show some compassion. Of course, the person who cheats is the bigger asshole but will be blamed less than the person one cheated with by the person one cheated on. That's just human nature, to not hate what you love, and want to blame someone else, anything else.

The confrontation was inevitable but different than I'd imagined. It came exactly a week after she told him. It was the first cold day of autumn and drizzling just enough to be annoying, and for me to wish I'd worn a scarf, when I arrived home from the grocery store to see him standing by my stoop. I saw him first and felt a strain in my chest, even considered ducking off, but then gathered myself and walked toward the showdown, almost relieved to get it over with.

He looked more embarrassed than angry, which led me to believe we were going to have an adult conversation, but I wasn't sure what was lurking underneath his cool diffidence. He put out his hand which would force me to rest my grocery bags on a knee to shake. It was awkward. He almost withdrew it when he realized this, but then thought taking it back might be misinterpreted, so let it linger like a dead bird until I did a quasi-crunch to balance the bags, and shook his hand.

"Hey."

"Hey."

Silence.

"Why don't you come in? It's pretty awful out here."

"No, it's okay."

The skin around his eyes was translucent and I could make out little blue veins that seemed to shiver with blood. His face was already a portrait one finds in albums of the old dead. He started to say something but then stopped as we looked at each other, and I had the strange feeling he might hug or murder me and it wouldn't make much difference to him.

"I forgive her."

I waited for him to say more.

"Tell her I forgive her."

I looked at him until I realized he was finished.

I nodded.

He gave me another look, and I felt this weird Jesus vibe and thought he was about to tell me he forgave me too, but he didn't. He turned and walked off, his shoulders reaching for his ears and his hands firmly in his overcoat pockets.

I went upstairs and sat at the kitchen table. Why'd he come to tell me that he forgave her? For me to tell her. Why not just tell her himself? It made little sense until I came to the conclusion this gesture wasn't meant to tell her anything. His message was to me. That I hadn't gotten the best of him. If he were angry, upset, jealous, it'd mean having to accept that I'd won the battle for his girlfriend's heart. I don't think he could've lived with that. It wasn't a snobby thing. That I wasn't of his class (just a measly college teacher etc.). I think he would've acted the same if I were a Dupont or Vanderbilt. He couldn't help thinking I might be gloating over the victory, and he wanted me to feel I hadn't won because he wasn't fighting. It was odd, but I was appreciative of it. And even though he was fake-walking off his imagined battlefield, I was fairly sure he wasn't going to tell anybody or have me fired, which was nice, considering I was getting used to this job and didn't have many other options. He finished out the semester in my class, though they no longer sat together, doing the minimum to get by. Objectively, he deserved a C+/B-, because his papers were not horrible; they were observant and polished, he had read the books, but there was no enthusiasm or anything that set him apart. He was adequate. When it came time to grade him, I gave him a B, thinking I was generous; not knowing I'd just given a courtesy B to someone who'd become the most famous student I ever had.

*　*　*

Two years after she graduated, I published my first novel, quit the teaching job and we got married and moved to New York. The truth was we were in love, very much; and though I have little faith in marriage, I allowed it to happen, mostly because she got pregnant, and how I thought she felt about it. A few weeks after the positive test, I detected a veil of sorrow fall over her, and I thought it was because she wanted to be married when she gave birth. Perhaps she was more traditional than I thought. When I pressed her on this, she admitted she wasn't sure why she was feeling down, but that yes, she'd prefer to be married. I sought out her father to ask permission, which I did at The Union Club in New York City. With an air of suspicion, he ordered us two scotches and said okay. A few weeks later, I was sheepishly presented with a prenuptial agreement forced on her by her parents. Rather than insulted, I was relieved, as this would hopefully ease remaining doubts of my intentions. (I think I barely made it over the line with them. My novel was just successful enough to nudge me into the acceptable column; her mother could say with wide eyes at the club, *She's marrying a writer*, as if she'd brought home an exotic bird from the Galapagos.)

We got married on a singingly beautiful day near the water on their Connecticut property, and everything went off pretty well. Our parents, though vastly different, even got along; it was a happy night, most of us dancing till 4 a.m., and then we were off on our honeymoon to Puerto Rico; and I felt that beyond a few yearly family holidays, we were free. On our way to the "Island of Enchantment," the rising sun blaring through the airplane window onto my wife's beautiful, if hungover, face, I felt a wonderful calmness which had nothing to do with the spiritual legalese of marriage, but more that my life was heading toward the kind of stability where I could love and work without having to give much thought to anything else. Plus we were going to be parents; and though I would've been uneasy with any past girlfriend, I had faith in my new wife's values, her goodness, that she'd be an amazing mother; and no matter how much I faltered, she'd keep us on a path toward whatever the best in life can offer.

She got a job on the Lower East Side as a social worker, so we rented an apartment in the East Village on 9th and Avenue B. Tompkins Square Park spread out below our scuffed windows like a carpet of colors and surprises. We were happy there, continuing our life of work and quiet pleasure; and when our first boy was born, despite the cranky sleeplessness and increased bickering most veteran parents don't warn new parents about, we survived, still loving each other and, even more, loving our little boy, who of course we believed to be the most handsome, funniest, spectacular child ever born. A year and a half later came another boy, and as luck would have it, he too was the most singular, incredible child. What were the chances of that! In the meantime, I'd followed up my first novel with a second, which had just enough critical and commercial success to keep us humming along without much financial worry. My wife had paused her work at Henry Street Settlement to get her master's in sociology at NYU. And so we'd both work mostly from home, breaking for sloppy take-out lunches with our little ones. We were a happy family.

It was around this time we started seeing him on television. He'd been writing for a right-wing political newspaper and was invited from time to time to amplify those positions on major networks. On TV (lights, camera, make-up), he seemed less uptight, more agreeable, smiling in between looks of glossy outrage at what he deemed "feely" political correctness, spending plans that didn't reduce the budget or policies that gave what he considered "handouts" to minorities. He was nauseating, but it was all so theatrical and silly, clearly for ratings, that no serious person could actually care. Not near the vile froth he'd work himself up to over the next two decades. He was like a ham and cheese sandwich smothered in mayonnaise. Almost comforting.

We kind of marveled at him on TV. When he was on, my wife would call from the other room and we'd both watch, giving each other funny looks. Mine mocking, hers quizzical. As time went on, he appeared more frequently, eventually obtaining his own show; and soon, we stopped watching as he became a daily fixture in the lives of millions of Americans.

When you have children, the years—no longer measured by specific dates like birthdays but by your children's height and intellectual milestones—speed along faster. We were content with our two boys, had no need for more kids, though I'd always imagined having a girl. A part of me was happy we hadn't, because I think my average parental worries would've compounded enormously. Internet, perverts, drunk teenage idiots on Spring Break . . . Of course, anything horrible that could happen to a girl might happen to a boy, but as my grandmother used to say, *With a boy you worry about ONE penis, with a girl ALL of them.* I was relieved I wouldn't have to answer the door with a bat and menacing smile. I heard from friends, though, that a father's love for his daughter is something extra (what, I couldn't imagine). It's just different, they'd say. All the same, my love for my boys—how could I love any more than that? I'd often look into their eyes and tell them they'd always be my babies, even when they were grandfathers; and I'd cover them in kisses, to their shrieks. She and I were fine as well, most of our time spent enjoying our children. And we were in agreement with the discipline we doled out, as the last thing we were going to do was raise spoiled brats. Luckily, both boys, though different, loved animals (and each other) and were mostly kind, non-pushers, so we felt half our work was done without doing anything.

* * *

Who can say the exact moment a marriage falls apart? Surely some can because there's a specific incident, an infidelity or betrayal that reveals a divide one never knew existed. Suddenly the covers are yanked back, and you realize the foundation you thought was solid was just airy fantasy and it's a miracle you didn't fall into the abyss sooner. That's not the way it was for us. It was more like continental plates imperceptibly grinding further and further apart until you wake up and there's an ocean between you. An ocean of prickly unsaids, lazy disinterest, and a dwindling lack of enthusiasm for bonds once cherished. As our children grew up and went to college, she spent more time looking into her phone after dinner, the news, a recipe, a yoga class. And I stopped caring as I dissolved into my own distractions, a new TV series, aimless contact with forgotten friends. Before dinner, we'd plan to watch a movie together, but the shiny, brain-pulling magnets in our hands would call us back into our own diversions until we were too tired to do anything together but sleep. As my books piled up, I wouldn't share reviews or ask her opinion, and she'd stop recounting what happened at work—the personal stories that'd once moved us. Maybe we were tired. Maybe my youthful belief was right: marriage was for the birds, and not meant to last. After nineteen fairly happy years, and with an enviable lack of fuss, we divorced and remained in cordial contact over the boys, who were in college now, and too busy discovering who they were (and who they wanted to be with) to lose sleep over their parents' break-up, which would affect them minimally since they no longer lived at home, and never felt unloved by either of us.

Our divorce officially came through and was signed on the day Donald Trump was elected president. Becoming single at 50 is not the party you might expect, but it's still better than being married. I'd missed out on the dating app thing, but if you're a writer who's had a modest amount of success, you probably can get by without them. I did readings around the country, so there was never a shortage of dates with women who were certainly physically, and perhaps morally and intelligently, out of my league. I was lucky I didn't have to be alone though I often chose to be, more out of lazy dread at the prospect of getting to know someone, trade all those stories etc; and though I had a strong libido (compared to what or whom I don't know), the tug to stay home and watch TV usually won out over getting un-casually-casually dressed, picking a restaurant, texting, talking, and making out at a dive bar at the end of the night. At my most lazy, I'd order in a sensual massage, or visit one of those sad parlors (for what I told myself was mostly a massage, to assuage the guilt) to vary the necessary tedium of masturbation. Sounds dreary, I know, but despite the moral degradation for all involved, I still did it. I had fast sexual relief when I needed it, romance when I wanted it, and friendship when I missed it. Of course, my constant was work, but the creative, enjoyable stuff (I'm a writer who likes writing, shoot me) was only two hours in the morning. The rest of the day was rote: coffee with my agent, reading galleys, books, magazines.

Like many Americans during this era, I got swept up in politics. And naturally, as I watched more news, I saw more of him. Still (I can't not blurt this out anymore!) the biggest laugh was on me . . .

I don't know why she didn't call to tell me. And I do know very well why she couldn't. She knew how incomprehensible, upside-down-world-unlikely, plain impossible it would be to me. It would erase everything I thought I knew about human beings, humanity, her, us, life, anything at all. Still, I wish I'd found out from her.

High School Sweethearts Back in Step with a picture of them walking down Park Avenue holding hands with smiles on their faces, in black-tie after what I presume was a gala, her hair loose and blown back by the wind, as if she never gave a shit. Certainly didn't give a shit enough to tell me before everyone in New York, or possibly America, knew. When I called, she said they were just friends. When I called again, she admitted they were more than friends and that she wanted to be honest with me, though she'd lied two hours earlier. Six months later, they were living together. We are human. Unfathomable, every one of us.

Looking back now, I can't help feeling sorry for her having to tell me. I couldn't imagine having to call *me* and say she'd gotten back together with *him*. I would've preferred the rack. Someone we ridiculed. Or maybe I'd been the only one doing that; maybe I'd just assumed she felt the same way. Maybe I'd underestimated their bond, their roots, the strength of their entangled comforts. Maybe I was a horrible writer, didn't notice anything, even though it was my job to be observant. How could I not have known this was going to happen? Foreseen it somehow. A hint. No, I never had a fucking hint.

I received a letter a few days after the second phone call. Why? I think she questioned my sanity or she felt guilt, or she hadn't lost her charitable soul and believed I needed some sort of explanation. Of course she said it in a flowery way: *I had no hand in this. I had no choic*e. *Fate* etc., etc. In short, she said, *I'm not a bitch*. But c'mon.

* * *

This might have all turned out okay if it weren't for the boys. His influence on them. From her, I could let everything slide: the humiliation, the reshuffling of my understanding of the human spirit, etc. Fine. But him? That Country-Club-Man-Of-The-People influencing my kids? No.

It started with my eldest on one of my weekends during his junior year in college. A comment over the dinner table. Trump was being discussed, and at one point he said, "I think he's kind of funny." Six words. Jesus H. Christ. Might not seem like a big deal, maybe innocuous, in fact it could even be true, but that he said it sounded a million alarms. I should've stepped back, been cool; the worst thing you can give a teenager is some hard stance to rebel against. But I fucked up. I said, "Yeah, pretty funny, ripping kids out of their mother's arms at the border. Hysterical." My son shook his head and continued eating, not wanting to engage but agreeing that that was fucked up, while also letting me know there was probably more to it. Maybe it wasn't all black and white. Either way, I felt an icicle slide through my aorta.

Soon after that, there was the Pandemic, and he spent a lot of time isolating with his mother. And of course *him*, since he was working from home and lying about it, as usual. I saw my boys less during that year and a half, but we Zoomed twice a week, and I felt we hadn't lost any connection.

When things loosened up after the vaccine, my boys started spending more weekends at mine, and I noticed my eldest's style had switched from ripped T-shirts and sneakers to polo button-downs and boat shoes. One evening on his way out to meet friends, I noticed he was wearing a collared shirt over another collared shirt. I had to say, "What are you wearing?" He smirked and leaned in to give me a kiss goodnight. "Love you," he said, as he turned and walked down the hallway. Of course this is what always happens, but it's awful. I told myself,

THE REUNION

Don't push anything on him, but over the next few weekends, I'd bring up political issues sideways, in terms of morality not personality, to edge him toward an empathetic view (or at least gauge where he was), but he was tight-lipped. I couldn't tell if I was getting through.

Then the bomb exploded. The summer internship. Yes, procured by my star ex-student. When my son told me, to my credit, I remained calm (though he did ask if I was okay), but when I called her later that night, I lost it.

"Are you out of your mind?" I screamed into the phone.

"Calm down."

"Calm down? Your husband (Did I mention they got married?) is grooming my kid."

"Don't exaggerate."

"Exaggerate?! And what's all this religious shit? Taking our kids to church!"

She took a deep breath. She was trying hard not to hang up. "That's how I grew up."

I hung up. I was furious. I could lose her. But my kids, my boys? I had to lie down. My heart was beating so fast I thought I'd die, and I couldn't do that and leave them unprotected.

And what was his deal, my old courtesy-B student? His mother had left him when he was six to join a bunch of hippies, and no one likes to state the obvious, especially if you consider yourself a writer, but there it was.

My son was going to be working for him, listening to his buddies' jokes, having drinks with them after work, and there was nothing I could do about it.

* * *

I suppose now is as good a time as any to talk about it. That day. My youngest son was the one who called. Otherwise I might never have found out. My eldest had gone to hear Trump talk, whom he'd met in the green room a couple times before the show. He liked Trump. He brought my youngest to DC too. After Trump's speech, they'd walked with the rest of the crowd down to the Capitol. They had been toward the back of the throng but separated when it got out of control. My youngest called my eldest, but he didn't pick up. He called his mother, and she didn't pick up either, so he called me. He was scared. I spoke to my son as I watched it all on TV and couldn't believe the two people who mattered most to me were there. I didn't breathe as I watched the footage, looking for my son. I didn't see him. Turns out he had lost his cell phone; and when he couldn't find his brother, left to buy another one. An hour later, he called his brother, and they met up back at their hotel and watched it all on TV. I spoke to them as we watched. They had me on speaker, and I think they could tell I was choked up. I tried to let them know. I don't know if they understood.

* * *

A few weeks ago, I went back for my 35th reunion. I'm not sure why; I haven't been back since I stopped teaching. A woman in the administration who'd reached out to me over the years to do a reading (I always politely declined) emailed me out of the blue and asked if I was going. And weirdly, on a June day, I found myself driving on I-91 toward Connecticut. When I pulled up to the big parking lot, I saw lots of bright-looking parents in their 50s, many with teenage kids and some with youngsters, pulling straw bags and backpacks out of their trunks. Others were standing around on the lawn up ahead with drinks in their hands. I turned the car off and watched. The June sun was high and bright like it was meant to be. I thought of the parking lot from years ago when I got into his car. When she asked if I needed a ride. How different it all was, how the same it is. Most of the crowd from the parking lot had moved in toward the quad now, and I heard a mic turn on. The tops of the sycamores stirred with a light wind. I heard a cheerful, youthful, if slightly nervous, voice. "Welcome. Welcome, Class of 91."

Thank you to Anna David for her advice, and Katie Cosgrove for ushering this book into existence. Also to Juan Re Crivello for publishing some of the stories in earlier forms in *Gobblers & Masticadores*. Another big thank you to those who read the manuscript along the way: Thomas and Katherine Moffett, Valentí Gómez-Oliver and Enrico Pellegrini. Finally, deep gratitude and thanks to Nicole Burdette for her loving attention to these stories and decades of friendship.

Made in the USA
Middletown, DE
11 November 2024